Hellsong Series

Infidels: Cris

CONVALESCENCE

SHAUN O. MCCOY

SISYPHEAN PUBLISHING

This is a work of fiction. The damnation portrayed in this novel is fictitious, and similarities between it and any actual damnation are strictly coincidental.

Convalescence

Editor-in-Chief: Gabrielle Olexa
Associate Editors: Kitty Garner, Andrew Anderson, Justin Williams, Meredith Oliver

Title art: Dusan Arsenic
Title Layout: Paul Mavis

A Sisyphean Publishing Book

Http://hellsongseries.com

ISBN-13: 978-0692904404 (Sisyphean Publishing)
ISBN-10: 0692904409

First Edition March 2017

Printed in the United States of America

0 9 8 7 6 5

This book is for Lila Klinck

Convalescence

OTHER WORKS BY SHAUN O. MCCOY

From Neostoicism: Philosophia

Beauty is unbearable. It drives us to despair, offering for a minute the glimpse of an eternity we should like to stretch out over the whole of time.
—*Camus*

There is no evil like Eden.
—*Infidel*

Once more I reach up through the darkest depths and grab with my outstretched hand a single silver strand of wakefulness. It cuts deeply into my palms as I pull myself, bit by bit, hand over hand, into consciousness.

I'm in a dim room.

"It's okay," she tells me.

"Myla?" I ask.

I'd been sent to save Myla by a God I only half believed in. Myla's sister had told me so, sitting at the foot of my old world deathbed. And I'd found Myla. And we'd fallen in love. But something happened after that. Something I can't think about.

Her bobby pin. Her red hair. Her tearful face as she

reached out to me, begging me—

"I'm not Myla."

Myla had laughed when she'd seen me there, beaten by those devil men. She had stolen and poisoned my son.

Fuck her.

"Cris," the voice says. "Sweetheart. You're safe."

"I'm not."

"Do you want to talk about it?"

She coddles me like I'm a baby. My head is in her arms. I feel her abdomen against my face. It's firm, muscled, like a man's, only she's so tiny. It's El Cid. I'm safe. Somehow she'll fix it. I don't have to remember. I can just relax.

But relaxing is a mistake. My insides loosen, and I feel the pressure of my bruised innards against my sutured asshole.

My memories flood back into me, choking me with the pain of losing my son and the humiliation of being raped, and kicked . . . and mocked.

She holds me through the torrent.

I cry like a fucking bitch.

She wakes me. Feeds me. Gives me water.

As the days pass, shitting becomes easier, and my insides begin to feel solid again.

"You need to sleep, Cris."

But I lay there, eyes wide open. And really, what's the difference between the stilling and sleep. Not much. Except Shy is there when I sleep. Melvin is there. The twitching corpse of Fellman is there.

"We have your pack, Cris. Aren't you glad to have your things back? We saved them for you."

I don't care about my things.

She regrets saving me. I can see it in her eyes. I'm useless now.

Q is at the door.

No. He can't see me like this. Not like this.

"Go, Q," El Cid says.

"You don't understand, Cid," his deep voice echoes in my hollow sleeping chamber. "You don't know the bond between us. I'd die for him. He'd die for me."

Just go, Q.

There is a pause.

"He's been in here for days."

"I do understand, Q. I know Cris loves you. But you can't support him right now because he's ashamed. He just lost his son. He's been violated. He needs time."

I hear some shuffling. Q is in the room, a brilliant light behind him, silhouetting him, casting his shadow onto me. He steps closer.

He can't come closer. He can't.

"Go!" I screech.

He pauses, indecisive. It's hard to see his face in the

dim light, but there's pain on it.

"*Go!*"

Q's hurt, stunned. El Cid is pushing him.

"I'm sorry, Q," I say, and I can hear the fucking tears in my pathetic voice. "Please go. Please."

And he's gone.

She wakes me. Feeds me. Gives me water. Takes away my waste.

"I loved her, Cid."

"Who?"

Myla.

"The woman who captured you? Who we rescued you from."

"Yes." Her too.

"It's okay, Cris. That's natural. It's okay to break every once and a while. We'll make sure you anneal."

I don't know that word. I don't care to.

"Sometimes I want her to rescue me, Cid. Sometimes I want to be hers."

I can see Shy's brilliant red lips. I can sense her displeasure—and am assaulted by that memory where her oh-so-perfect face lolled to one side, eyes glazed over as the shadows of skeletons flickered across her features.

"Well you can't be hers. You're mine at the moment."

"But you don't really want me."

"She doesn't really want you either. Cris, I want what's best for you."

"I don't deserve that."

"Everyone deserves that."

"No."

"Yes."

"I miss him, Cid. I miss him so much."

"Aiden?"

"Yes."

"I know."

I can't tell her. She thinks Aiden is dead. He *is* dead, but he still moves. He still suffers. He probably still kills. At least he's alive in some way, right? In undeath?

I'm breathing easier, but my thoughts become consumed with my lost son.

He'd be alive in *some way* no matter what, in the next Hell. It's just worse now. Had he died I could have rested easy, hoping against hope that he was in Sheol, wishing he'd found a harbor in the storm of Hell. I'd have fantasies about dying and finding him some day.

But this is shittier.

Now I know he's alive. And I know what he'll do. He'll find people, kill them, and make them suffer more as he ushers the beaten souls deeper into this abyss. Or will he? He said he wanted to help them.

Fingers are on my forehead, brushing back my hair. My back tightens.

Whose fingers?

Cid's fingers. "Do you remember, on the boat, before Soulfall?"

I nod.

"You told me something, then," she whispers.

I did. I told her. I told her. I told her words I should have saved for Myla.

Her tiny lips touch mine. They're firm, but she uses them gently, caressingly.

"I love you too, Cris. Not in the way you love me, but in the way *I* love people. Do you understand?"

I nod. "More."

"I am powerful, Cris. I can bring you back to life."

But my soul is as dead as my son's.

She kisses me again. I feel the rush of my blood in my ears, and for once it's not from anger or sorrow. The music is only in my mind, but it sings. Her lips are still gently caressing, coaxing, exploring, loving, whispering something. I struggle to hear it.

"Again," I whisper into her mouth.

"I love you," she says.

"Again."

"I love you."

"Again."

"I love you, Cris. I love you. I love you." And then, "You are not alone."

She kisses me a little harder, and my heart pounds, and I need it. I need *this*. I need it more than I've ever needed anything before—more than health, or love, or salvation. Her tiny tongue makes tiny circles in my mouth. I push against her, kissing harder, faster, and she responds. I hear her breath quicken as her lips work, sucking, opening, closing, moving, attempting in some sensual way to devour me. She's a passionate devil now, her hands around me, searching over me, pressing against my body.

I sit up as fast as I can, bruising our lips together. I taste blood in my mouth, her blood, from her lip, and it excites me. Her fingers find my belt, and I can barely wait for her to free me. There is no foreplay. I enter her, when she's still not quite ready, forcing my way—bit by bit—through the friction because I cannot stop. I know it must hurt her. I know it must be painful, but I'm insane. It must be now. And suddenly she's ready and the friction is gone.

Then it *is* now. And I fuck her. I fuck her so hard we're sliding back across the stone. She raises her hands to keep me from slamming her head into the wall, and I beat her body against the stone again and again and again and faster and faster and faster with all the passion I've ever felt because the only alternative is the sick, sick pain which lies at the bottom of my maddened mind.

My fingers grope her still clothed body, pressing her shirt into her firm tit, squeezing her at the nipple. And then my hands find their way along her waist to where I feel her skin beneath her shirt and I shove the cloth up and I hunch down because she's so tiny I can barely reach her breast with my mouth and I suck and I suck and I suck until I can taste her sweat.

And I still cannot stop.

I need this.

I need this more than anything I've ever needed before.

I crave this.

I crave this more than anything I've craved before.

"Again," I say.

"I love you."

I ram my lips into hers as I fuck her.

I lean back. "Again!"

"I love you."

"Again."

"I love you, Cris. I love you. I love you."

Then I feel her clenching against me, again and again. And she begs and croons and cries and shouts. And I'm not far behind.

All is still.

I find myself lying next to her, in the crook of her arm, my head resting against her small shoulder.

"You are not alone," she says.

And somehow, on some level, that's what all people need to hear. Particularly the damned ones.

In a moment of clarity, I realize I didn't believe her when she first said it. She would say anything to make me feel better, I'd thought. But she's an infidel. She's meant every damn word she's said.

It strikes me.

I'm not alone.

And then, just as quickly, comes the following realization.

Aiden is.

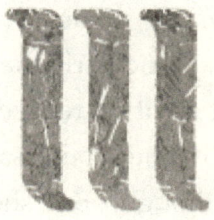

I awaken.

There's some dried dyitzu jerky lying on a woodstone plate next to a water-filled stone cup. I take a few bites. The jerky is tough, salty, and dry. I dip it into the water to loosen it up a little. Chewing takes quite a while, and gristle gets caught in my back molars.

I drain the glass.

Aiden is gone.

How do I deal with this?

I stand up and test my ankle.

It's sore in its wrapping, but it supports my weight well and is surprisingly close to pain free. Maybe the injury wasn't as bad as I thought. Maybe it was just a sprain this whole damn time—or maybe I'd lain, soulfucked, in this dark room for so long the break had healed.

I limp over to the door.

Light creeps in along the floor from the room beyond. I think the door is of infidel make, or it at least appears so, with woodstone planks bound evenly together with iron. The knob, which is a rare thing to find in Hell, turns with ease. The door swings open, issuing a long creak. The squeal of the ancient hinges decreases in pitch as the last of the door's momentum dies away—then all is silent.

I step out into the hallway, my bare footstep slapping against the warm stone. I close the door behind me, its hinges' protest punctuated by the thud of woodstone on stone and the small click of the latch.

I'm in a hallway. There are about four rooms with similar doors to my left before the hallway dead ends. To my right are a dozen more rooms, and the passage opens up into some larger area. It has carpet, and I remember crawling on all fours, barking like a dog before Fellman took me.

I sink to my haunches, covering my face with my hands.

Come on, Cris, you can't think about this stuff.

A shadow falls over me. It's Q.

For a split second, I worry he might be angry with me after I'd so carelessly shouted at him, but no, there is a wide grin on his face—such an uncharacteristic smile from the stoic man.

He helps me up and catches me in a hug. "You're out."

I hug him back. "Yeah."

"I knew the stilling wasn't going to get you, Cris," he says. "I knew it."

He knew it. I didn't. I still don't. I feel it calling me, in the back of my mind. And it is indeed a stillness. That name seems so apt now.

For a moment, though, I bask in the friendship— and then he releases me, stepping back.

"I'm okay," I lie.

"Come on, brother," he says to me, "let me show you the study."

The study is well-lit by warm light emanating from certain ceiling stones. There's burnished wood furniture, easy chairs and couches and a bookshelf with bona fide, honest-to-God books. A clock adorns one wall, one hand dutifully ticking off the seconds while the others wait their turn.

"Where are we?" I ask.

Q purses his lips. "An infidel safe chamber. We think it was built by Archades, an elder Infidel Friend who's likely dead."

I start to ask him a question, but I don't really know which one to start with.

"Come on," Q says. "I'll show you around. Staying

in a safe chamber for *too* long is dangerous, you're bound to draw a Minotaur, but we're a couple months away from having to worry about that. This is going to be our home for a while so we can get you . . ."

"Healed?" I ask.

"No," Q answers. "Trained. While we get you trained. We've got to give you some concepts and some basic skills you can work on for when we go back into Hell."

That's not the real reason, and he and I both know it. The real reason is that I need to get my head on straight after getting mind fucked by Igraine's people, and I have to do that *before* they're willing to take me back out into Hell. That makes sense. Right now, I'd just get them killed.

Q walks out of the room and beckons me onward.

"Good," I say.

IV

Q leads us into an Eden, then stops me with an upraised hand.

I cannot process what I'm seeing.

"There is a danger here, Cris," he whispers. "An insidious one."

He must be lying. Hell has no sanctuary, this I know . . . but this place is safe—this place is heaven.

Skystone veins, effusing a calm, golden glow, line the ceiling in even rows, each as thick as my arm, each running the length of the hundred-yard chamber. A waterfall issues smoothly from the far wall, filling Eden cavern with the sound of gently rushing water even as it forms the river which meanders gently across the room.

Past one riverbend, a half-hidden waterwheel turns smoothly behind some brineberry bushes, its languid spin powered by the soft current. Hungerleaf and mika trees sprout up from the soft loamy ground, their branches reaching upward in rapture to the luminescent skystone. Green sprouts of devilwheat double for grass, and sinfruit vines crawl up the walls, sagging under the weight of their ripening fruit.

The air is cool, but humid. A path formed out of marble flagstones crosses the chamber, bridging the river with a simple arch. Benches, carved with floral and pagan designs, invite me to sit near the top of devilwheat-covered knolls or under the shade-casting canopy of hungerleaf trees.

My heart is rent by this tranquility. How was I to know to prepare for something like this? How could I know this kind of pain existed?

This Eden is so beautiful that it tears my insides back apart. It's a different kind of agony, a loss so profound and so very different from the empty pit my fallen son left in the hollow of my chest, or the hole Melvin had dug out in my lower intestines. This place has everything in it my damned soul wishes for.

I cover my eyes to hide my weakness.

"Be not embarrassed," Q assures me. "Many men, men greater than you and I have wept upon seeing one of these. But before it overwhelms you, before hope takes root in your soul, I need you to listen to me, Cris.

Can you listen?"

Numbly, I nod.

"The Infidel warns us that there is no evil like Eden. Peace can destroy a warrior as surely as war. Fortune can break a man as surely as misery. Success can destroy a heart as surely as failure. In Hell, this is especially so.

"This place, these places, they were built by men, not the Architect, but they form a trap as deadly as any Hell has ever devised. Eden will call to you, tempt you, cheat you of your will. It will sing to you its song—and you'll lose your sense of time. You'll forget that there are others who suffer outside these walls, others who need your help. You'll forget that staying here is what draws them . . . the Minotaurs, the Nephilim, the Archdevils and their stonewights. The fallen angels and the banshees. The Icanitzu lords and the Dezendyitzu. They can sense when a man stays put for too long. That's why they're drawn to cities. That's why they're drawn to camps. But a haven like this, it calls to them even more loudly.

"Who knows how they can sense it? Maybe it's the stillness of the air. Maybe it's that no devils have traversed this way. We've tried many things to keep them from finding chambers like this. Many, many things. But always, they come. Always.

"You'll be resting, you'll feel sure it's been too long—that for some reason, this place, this time, is the one where you'll get eternal peace. But they'll come, and softened by that peace, you'll die.

"Do you understand me, Cris?"

I hear his words, but I don't want to understand them.

"Do you?" he repeats. "You can convince yourself of their truth later, but for now, I just need to know that you hear me."

I take my hand away from my eyes and look again at the chamber, at this living embodiment of all that has ever been taken from me. "I hear you."

Q leads me out of Eden cavern quickly, and I'm thankful that he does. I do want to go back, though. I want to sit on one of those benches, smell the air, listen to the water, and daydream about some meaningless thing. But if I did . . .

My arms are shaking, and my step is unsteady. "More," I say.

Q gives me one of his patented quizzical looks, eyebrows raised into the furrows in his forehead.

"Show me more of this place," I say. "I want to know more about where we're staying."

Q is only to happy to oblige. "The river you just saw is the source of our grey water system," he says, pointing behind us. "It flows through to our baths."

I stop in the hallway. "Baths," I mumble.

Q nods. "It's an infidel thing. We try to keep a

good understanding of technology. Plumbing is one of those technologies. One day, Cris, we're going to beat Hell. We'll need all those skills again, just like we did when we were the ancients."

Q leads me back to the study and then to the hallway with our bedrooms. He stops at one door and opens it.

I can tell it's a latrine, but as far as latrines go, it smells pretty nice.

"This is where we've been dumping your bed pan," Q tells me. "I think Cid would appreciate it if you started taking care of that yourself."

I nod, and for a brief moment, I feel euphoria. Maybe it's an after effect of the Eden room. Maybe it's that I realize I'm healed enough to shit on my own. Maybe it's just that purist form of denial which is so often the harbinger of an upcoming mental breakdown.

Q smiles. "You're going to want to use that thing in the corner, by the sink. It's a bidet. You ever heard of one before?"

It looks like a cross between a sink and a toilet.

I frown. "French, isn't it?"

Q shrugs. "There's no toilet paper, so if you want to be civilized, apparently French is your only option. You good?"

"*Oui oui*," I say.

Q chuckles.

It feels odd to have made a joke.

I lean over and look down the black stone toilet. It's like one from the old world, but instead of flushing, it simply has a hole with a river at the bottom.

"Don't worry," Q says. "This water doesn't mix with the baths."

At the end of the hall is a small archway which leads into a cramped spiral staircase. We can only go through single file and Q has to duck to use it.

"You sure Archades built this thing?" I ask.

"Not sure, why?"

The hellstone of the stairwell scrapes my shoulder as we walk down it.

I stop. "It's small."

Q's deep laughter echoes about in the tight confines. "Maybe they built it for Cid? We were at the top, the fourth level. Are you good to see the third?"

Ever so gingerly, just as when I first put weight upon my ankle, I test my emotional state.

"Yes," I say. "I think so."

On the third level, there's a kitchen, complete with some kind of stove, knives and chopping boards, an opening to a river cellar, and a 1930s looking silver-fauceted sink.

"I've never seen a sink dropped from the old world," I mention.

Q shakes his head. "I'm sure it's happened, but this one is infidel made."

Jesus, but it looks like, well, like it was

manufactured. Heaven ain't far from a place like this.

He takes me down to the river cellar. It's cool here, almost unnaturally so. The stores are extensive. They keep stacks of sliced meat behind a set of cubbies on the second floor.

"We treat the meat with an extract of knowledge fruit," Q explains. "It draws out the corpsedust. In theory, if properly treated, the meat will never rot."

"Is that true?" I ask.

He shrugs. "Can't be sure. Hard to know how meat made thousands of years ago was treated."

They have other things as well. Hound milk. Honey. Devilwheat. Brineberries. Hungerleaf tea leaves. Spider eggs. Everything.

"You ready for level two?" he asks.

I'm not. The weight of Q's joviality is too heavy for me to bear much longer—but again, I lie. "Sure."

Our second level has the baths. They are Romanesque, a combination of pool and sauna.

"This takes energy from the main battery," Q says, pointing to three levers on the wall. "The levers control the baths."

"Battery?" I mumble.

Q smiles. "A kinetic battery. It's pretty much just a big rock on a chain. That's what the waterwheel is charging." He motions back to the levers. "This one adds heated water to the pool. This one steams up the room, and this one adds cool water. As you can see, the excess water pours out through there. It will try and flush itself every day or so."

"Automatically?"

"Yes. It's set up with gears. There's a clock run by the same system in the study, if you didn't notice."

The second level also has a periscope.

"There's a lot of crystal walls surrounding this complex," Q explains. "The scope does a good job of letting us see what's going on outside. We can spy on Hell. The viewing is passive. The view ports are completely dark, so the devils can't see in. The light of their chambers is reflected through a tube to the scope. You can choose which port to look out of by spinning it. Don't worry, you'll have time enough to try it out later."

We then travel down to level one, which has another toilet.

"Our waste is slowly introduced into the river," Q tells me. "That way, we're less likely to attract a Minotaur. This level also has the armory."

Q points toward a steel door.

"What's that?" I ask, pointing to what looks almost like an old world breaker box.

The box's door has the sign of the infidel etched into it.

Q puts one hand on the metallic door. "It's a failsafe. If someone finds us, we can use this to make sure no one gets what's in this room."

I ask the obvious question. "How?"

"It buries the armory under a thousand feet or so of rubble. Then a call goes out so, in theory, a high ranking Infidel Friend will come in the next few months with a group and recover it."

"In theory?"

"This base might be forgotten, or so far away as to be unreachable."

This level also has the training room. It's a fifty foot by fifty foot space. There are mats stacked up on one side and a wall of cubby holes filled with practice swords, bows and arrows, guns, and a ton of things I don't recognize.

"The training room is nice," Q says. "Let me show you the basement. Don't worry, it's just one room."

The basement is an observation room, sealed shut by a metal hatch which looks like it came out of a submarine. A small ladder leads us down into its tight confines.

"Stay quiet," Q whispers. "It's soundproofed, but one can never be too careful. You can whisper, but make sure not to shout."

Quiet is something I long for. My head is aching from the energy it takes to be around a normal person.

Three of the basements walls are made of black hellstone. The fourth is made of ironglass. Beyond the ironglass is a clear crystal wall. Though the chamber beyond that crystal is dim, it is nothing like the complete darkness of the basement. That way, like with the scope, we can see out, and no one can see in.

"It's perfect," I say softly.

"The watch room?"

Yes. Because it's quiet and dark. "No, the whole thing."

And that's what kills me. In the old world this was nothing special. We had this level of safety every minute of every day. Safety, food and water. I would like to drag one of those people from above—one of those people who think they're suffering. I want to grab their shirt and pull them up to me. I want to look them dead in the eye. Tell me, motherfucker, tell me you're unhappy. All that shit, your work stress, your backstabbing friends, your fucking ex-lovers, they're all extra. You have what you need.

In Hell, this can't last. If we stay, sooner or later a Minotaur will find us. It will gather an army of devils. They will surround this place. They will dig their way in and slaughter us. All our efforts, all this fighting, and the best we can manage is to have something almost as good as the old world for a few weeks.

I really am damned.

I look out through the ironglass wall to the Hell beyond. My son is out there. Alone. His soul twisted and tainted by wightdust. His mind confused.

I walk up to the wall and touch the glass.

Q rests his hand on my shoulder.

He wants us to go, but I'm not ready.

He leans forward and whispers in my ear. "Feel free to stay and keep watch. I'm heading out. I'm going to try and stock up the armory and make sure no devils are on our trail."

"Okay," I whisper back.

Wait. He's going out there?

He can't do that! What if he finds Aiden? Will El Cid still love me if she finds out I lied to her? If she finds out I created and protected a wight?

Well, she wouldn't kill me, I don't think. But there's no way she'd keep training me, and I'm days away from any city—if I could even find the way.

Damn.

Q silently ascends the ladder. I need to tell him. I need to bare all. I need his help to keep my failure a secret from Cid. But I'm exhausted. Later. I can be honest later.

He unseals the hatch with a few twirls of the submarine-style lock.

He won't keep a secret from Cid, though. Not because he doesn't love me, but because he's a good person.

And I'm not.

My noble friend disappears through the hole above. There is the ever-so-soft sound of the padded hatch closing.

I stare out into the room beyond, into the Hell that,

for the moment at least, I'm not a part of. I feel helpless.

Well, God, you sure made certain that we were awful small creatures, didn't you? Awful small.

About a minute or so later, on the other side of the ironglass, I watch Q traverse the small natural chamber. I'm not sure if he's silent as death, or if the soundproofing is working. I expect him to nod or wave, but he gives me no signal before disappearing into the wilds.

Probably infidel procedure or something, in case he's being followed.

I revel in the sudden loneliness, closing my eyes against the small stress headache and massage my temples with my fingers. Breathing the cool air feels . . . feels . . .

My ankle aches a little. There may still be some

swelling because the boot Jessica'd made me is tight on my right foot. The floor here is cooler than in the other chambers, and I let the cold seep into my body.

The wheel lock of the hatch above me spins. It occurs to me that a devil might have broken into our complex, but I don't care. Let it come. I'll just enjoy the cool stone. I hear boots on the rungs of the ladder.

A grey overcoated figure sits down next to me.

It's Nebuchadnezzar.

Why couldn't he just leave me alone?

After all we've been through, I'm amazed that his overcoat seems to be in perfect condition. My clothes, on the other hand, are shit.

The Aryan necromancer isn't looking at me; he's staring out through the glass.

"You owe me," he says.

"Oh?"

"I'm the one they had lug your pack around while you were gone."

"Thanks."

"Aiden?" he asks in a whisper, a tinge of German in his accent coloring the name.

I call that his honest voice. His other voice was the one coached by the Nazis in order to make him better able to integrate with allied soldiers.

"Dead," I deliver the half-lie quietly.

"I know. I meant to be asking something else. Perhaps you're worried that he didn't love you?"

I think about this. Nebuchadnezzar is very close to being on point. If Aiden was dead, completely dead, that's probably one of the things that'd be on my mind. I'm not sure how much I want to share my feelings with this monster, but right now I think I'd be tempted to talk to a dyitzu just for the company.

"Yeah," I say.

"And what else?"

I shift, straightening against the cold stone wall, suddenly aware of how transparent my lies could be. "Isn't that enough?"

I want to tell him. God help me, I want to tell him everything. About how my son turned. About those black eyes. About him waiting in the darkness, not to kill me, but to convert me. About how he'd wanted to raise the corpse of my ex-lover and make us some kind of unwholesome undead family.

"We can pretend it is," Neb says. "I don't think you understand how lovable you are."

Fellman had known.

His words were meant as a compliment, but considering they came from a corpsefucker, I'm not sure how much they count. "Thanks, I guess."

"I'm very serious, Cris. I don't think you realize the effect you have on people. You're very determined. You won't stop. You're so driven that someone you love knows you'll come to save them. That's something nice to have."

I shrug.

"You're not like Cid or Q," he says. "You're more like, well not really like this, but like the Infidel, in a way. When I met him, he didn't judge me either. He didn't think of me as . . ."

"As a God damned Nazi war criminal complicit in genocide? One who'd used that knowledge to raise and fuck corpses?"

His jaw clenches for a moment, and then relaxes. "Yeah. Like that."

I feel the heat of my blood in my veins.

I stand. "You want to know why that is?"

He looks up at me, his blue eyes curious.

"Well I'll fucking tell you. I needed you, Nebuchadnezzar. I *needed* you. I'd have pretended anything. I'd have acted in any way. I'd even pretend to forgive a son of a bitch like you to save my son. And I did pretend. You sick fuck. You corpsefucker. You have no idea how disgusted I am at you. At what you did. At all the people you and your friends killed."

I'm breathing hard, and my face is flushed. But I'm sick of this. I'm sick of seeing Melvin's squint-eyed face when I go to sleep at night. I'm sick of watching my son in pain. I'm sick of lying to this arrogant bastard. And he's smiling the smile that touches his eyes.

He points to the ironglass. "We must be quiet," he whispers nonchalantly.

Oh, I know better. My words are cutting him. I

want to see him bleed—and I know how to make that happen.

"And you know what else?" I ask.

He doesn't respond.

"I *did* lie to get you here. Eva is a lie, Neb. I don't know where she is. It was all bullshit. And I don't feel guilty because a person like you doesn't have a soul worth shit."

His mask shatters and I see his naked dismay. I feel glee. He turns his face away from me.

That's right, fuckhead. That's what I think of you. You thought this whole time—

"I know," he says.

Wait.

"What?"

"I know," Nebuchadnezzar repeats. "I knew you were lying then. But I *wanted* to believe you."

His voice sounds odd. Is he crying? Wouldn't that be a peach. Since this is the afterlife, I'm sure there are about six million people somewhere around here who'd want to be watching this.

"I told you," I say, remembering to keep my voice low, "all you Nazi fuckers have a hard-on for Eva."

His shoulders slump. "No, you don't understand." His German accent creeps back into his voice. "It's not because of Eva. I wanted to believe you because it gave me an excuse. An excuse to really do what I wanted to do. I saw your boy and I wanted to help him. I wanted to help you."

The feeling of joy I'd gotten at hurting him dies in my chest. Should I bother feeling guilty? I'd said something, in fact, I'd even lied a little, just to hurt him. I had heard a rumor about where Eva was. It was just a rumor, but it was something a man could try to follow up.

Neb had saved me. He'd worked with Cid and Q to rescue me. I owe him something.

"I don't know if I believe you," I tell him.

But I'm lying again. I do believe him.

He turns his head back around, finally, looking at me. He's got a mask back on. It's not that stupid smile of his. Nor is it the absolute look of unconcern I'd observed back at the Pole. No, this is something different. This is something close to Q and Cid's stoicism. Those fuckers can really rub off on people.

He stands up and faces me.

"I'm yours, if you will have me," Nebuchadnezzar whispers. "Your friend. Your soldier."

I gaze back out through the crystal. "I don't even know how to begin—"

Neb steps forward and grabs my shoulders. His eyes are wide, mad like they were on Soulfall. "But I do. I know where to start!"

I raise my eyebrows.

"You owe me, Cris. You were supposed to take me to Eva, but I don't care about that. The Infidel, Cris, the

Infidel. He can redeem me. He can absolve my guilt. That was the deal he made me. He wouldn't have offered it if he couldn't do it. Instead of going to Eva, take me to the Infidel."

I have to admit something to myself. I've wanted to like this guy for a while. It's just, well, I guess the Infidel is as good an excuse for me as Eva Braun was for him.

"Alright, Neb," I say. "Alright."

Neb had left me, and Q had long since returned to the complex—though he hadn't come down to see me in the watch room. I'm finally feeling the need to move. It's not that I've regained my spirits or my courage or anything, I'm just hungry.

I guess any need will do.

I climb up the ladder and spin open the lock.

As if to make me even more ravenous, someone is cooking, and I can smell whatever spices they're using even on the second level. I haven't smelled anything this good since the old world.

My mouth is watering, and just like I'm in some sort of cartoon, my stomach rumbles.

Q greets me from where he sits on a blanket covered chair. "Hey, I was just about to come get you. Cid's making some serious, serious dinner to celebrate you coming out of the pre-stilling."

"You think I'm out?"

"Aren't you?" Q asks, his face as stoic as ever.

I wonder about this, feeling the stilling roaring in some deep abyss just beneath me. "No."

"You can smell how good that is, though, right?" Q asks.

It feels good to feel hungry. "I can."

"Do *not* tell Cid about this. She might stop cooking."

A begrudging laugh is forced from me by Q's humor.

Together we walk up the stairs to the third level where the kitchen and dining room are. I see El Cid in the kitchen. She's up on her tippy-toes, grabbing something out of a cupboard. She grins at me.

I look around for Neb, but I don't think he's on this level.

I head back to the staircase.

"Hey?" Q stops me with a hand on my shoulder. "Where you going?"

"To find Neb," I tell him.

Q's eyes narrow. "He hasn't been eating with us."

I shrug.

Neb, Q and I sit in silence while El Cid brings in the food.

I've never seen anything like this before. There's a bowl of what looks almost like rice. I think it's actually the devilwheat seed, prepared in a certain way. The spicy dish is some sort of orange curry. It steams as El Cid puts it on the table. I take a whiff. My eyes water a little as the sting of its aroma clears my sinuses.

"Damn," I say.

She smiles at me, a kind of soft smile I've never seen from her before. "It's harpy curry."

"You can eat harpy?" I ask.

Q laughs. "You can. I wouldn't try it yourself though. If it's prepared wrong, you'll spend a fortnight vomiting."

The idea of eating something spicy makes me worried about the damage I'd taken internally, but I'd been shitting solidly for a few days now, so I try to dismiss the fear.

My hands are shaking, so I fold them in my lap.

Cid comes back, bringing rolls this time. Honestly, if I'd seen them in the old world, I wouldn't have thought anything of them. But here . . . the smell, it twists my soul. Jesus Christ, they smell like bread. Like actual bread. In her other hand is a bowl of something resembling lentils. The last dish she brings has slices of meat.

"Can you help me with the blood, bloodwater and

milk, Q?"

Her tone is . . . I can't quite place it . . . domestic. Her tone is domestic.

Tears start beading up in my eyes, not the bad kind, but I blink them back anyway.

Q nods and stands up. When he does so, the legs of his woodstone chair scrape across the floor. The sound is so familiar, so reminiscent of my life before damnation that it hurts.

Maybe Cid's right. Maybe, in some small way, I'm out of my funk.

This moment is so beautiful, so *right*.

Across the table, Nebuchadnezzar sits, stiff as a board.

Well, the moment's not right for all of us.

His face is expressionless, but his posture tells me how uncomfortable he is. That's odd. On our trip to the Erebus, being around the infidels hadn't bothered him at all.

I think about it and come up with a theory. Before, Neb hadn't cared about us. Now he does, so he's become vulnerable to shame.

Q and Cid return. Q has a corked stone cask and a decanter of milk. I assume it is hound's milk, since that's the only kind of milk I know of in Hell. Cid carries a glass container filled with something which looks like blood—only, it clearly hasn't coagulated, so it can't really be blood.

Cid pours us the bloodwater. "Now don't touch the milk and blood, that's for dessert."

"Is that really blood?" I ask.

She smiles. "It is. And the anticoagulant doubles as a sweetener. You're going to have to trust me on this one."

Q and Cid take a seat. They pause for a moment of introspection. It reminds me of how Christians pray before a meal, except it's subtly different. An infidel will thank those who saved their life, who trained them, who helped provide and prepare their meal. It was a moment to find one's center. I follow suit.

Thank you, Q, for believing in me. Thank you, Cid, for fucking me. Thank you, Infidel, for training these motherfuckers. And Archades, if this is a place you built, then I appreciate you too.

An awkward silence descends as we fill our plates.

I use a long-handled woodstone serving spoon to get some of the devilwheat rice, and then I follow Cid's example by putting the harpy curry on it. Again, it burns my eyes, but it's not at all unpleasant.

I pass the bowl of curry to Nebuchadnezzar, who takes it stiffly.

He isn't sharing in this moment, but I want him to. Hell, I *need* him to after I went off on him like that.

"So, Neb's decided to see the Infidel," I say.

Neb's head jerks up from the bowl.

Cid smiles warmly. "That's excellent."

She and Q look at Neb.

"It's true," he says. "Cris had agreed to take me to see Eva before, if you remember. We talked about that this morning and decided that wouldn't be very helpful. We thought it would be best if I saw the Infidel instead."

Q spoons some of whatever the lentil looking stuff is onto his plate. "Sounds like a good move. We're all a little messed up after Soulfall. He'll help you get yourself to where you want to be."

There's another moment of silence.

"I'm sorry about the racial slurs," Neb says.

Q grins. "Joke's on you, bud. I died in the Thirties."

Nebuchadnezzar lets out a deep, German guffaw.

El Cid is snickering too.

"What's so funny?" I ask.

"In the Thirties, nigger wasn't a racial slur," Nebuchadnezzar says. "Shitty word, but far from *casus belli*. I of all people should have known better."

I mull this over. "Yeah, but Q, you know what it means now."

He gives me a quizzical glance. "I'm not going to spend effort making myself vulnerable to racist misanthropes. Those men deserve no such weapon."

"He's got you there," the former Nazi cracks a smile.

Cid keeps laughing.

I admit to myself that maybe it is funny, in its own

fucked up way.

I take my first bite of the harpy curry.

My mouth metaphorically catches fire.

Holy shit.

Whoa.

Damn. That's hot.

I swallow it quickly. I feel it burn all the way down my throat. It hits my stomach, and starts burning there too. I cough a bit.

I reach for my bloodwater and take a couple of sips. The alcohol isn't exactly helping.

I feel sweat forming on my brow.

"Damn," I say, and my voice sounds hoarse.

Q laughs louder.

The harpy meat is chewy, tough and stringy, but the flavor is truly intense. I've never had anything like it on Earth or in Hell. Despite the burn, I take another bite. And another.

My eyes are watering like I'm a thirteen-year-old girl midway through a chick flick.

Neb and Q are having similar reactions. El Cid doesn't even blink, though. That tough-ass bitch.

El Cid passes me the lentils. "This will help cool your palate down."

I give myself a large heap. Eagerly, I take a bite.

Well, one thing's for sure, whatever those tiny little uneven spheres are, they aren't lentils. They are chewy, and the sauce which covers them has soaked into their outer shells. Those shells aren't hard at all, but sticky, and they catch on my teeth and on the roof of my mouth. The flavor of the sauce is garlicy. As I bite into one, I discover they all have something crunchy in their centers.

"What the hell is this?" I ask.

Neb is chewing on them thoughtfully. "Wait, are these spider eggs?"

I turn to Cid. "No they're not!" I insist loudly.

She gives me a grim smile. "I'm afraid—"

I hold up a hand. "Please. Let me have a few more bites in ignorance."

It feels good to laugh again. To feel carefree.

"So, Q," Cid says around a mouthful of curry and what is definitely-not-spider-eggs, "you want to fill these guys in on what you found out there?"

Q swallows his food. "The good news is that there aren't any devils nearby. Archades, or whoever built this place, built it in the middle of a corpse hole. Corpses tend to keep dyitzu out, so that's been helpful. So far, I haven't seen anything to suggest a Minotaur."

"That's good," I say.

Q takes a sip of bloodwater before continuing. "Good indeed. I tried to find the Carrion born's scattered slaves, but the catacombs is almost impossible to track anyone through. I found a great many of Neb's skeletons, some of them still twitching. Good work, that."

Neb smiles. "Thank you."

Q finishes his bloodwater. "None of the Carrion born bodies are there. Not the priestess, the little lady, nor even the soldiers. Even that hound was gone."

The thought of Shy sets my heart pumping.

"They might have become corpses," Cid suggests.

Q shakes his head. "Unlikely. I bet Igraine's people came through and cleaned up, or maybe even some other Carrion tribe. We should be safe, but I'll keep an eye out. There was some possible danger, though. I found some interesting dead dyitzu on the banks of the Erebus."

"Is a dead dyitzu really all that dangerous?" I ask.

"They were killed alone, each one by a blade," Q answers. "Not a knife, I'm thinking, but probably a sword—a very sharp sword."

Shit.

My son. He'd slain dyitzu with Q's blade in order to feed me.

Neb grunts. "That is odd."

"I'd seen another dead dyitzu, killed in the same way, shortly after we escaped Soulfall," Q says, "but I'd figured Cris got it with my sword."

El Cid grimaces. "That was quite some time ago. This other body was more recent?"

Q nods. "Someone might still be following us."

Fuck. That *must* be Aiden. This safe chamber has to be very close to Soulfall.

Nebuchadnezzar frowns. "Another Infidel Friend, perhaps?"

"Din," I say, reaching for any idea that might distract from the truth, "the Carrion guy you fought, Q. He had a rapier, and you said you didn't find his body. Any chance he's alive?"

Q shrugs. "He could indeed be alive. The skeletons Neb raised were both nearly blind and inefficient fighters, even when compared to a corpse. Either you or Neb could be right. But I don't think so. The strikes don't seem to have been delivered by a skilled hand, and the cuts are not narrow and deep like a rapier's would be. Could be from an infidel that's wounded, perhaps. Or someone in training."

Neb is nodding.

Jesus fucking Christ. They're going to hunt down my son and kill him.

"Keith," El Cid says.

What?

"Keith?" I ask.

Q takes another bite of the curry and swallows it quickly. "Many in the Order have had access to Infidel training. It's not inconceivable to think that one of Keith's men has learned how to forge a lesser blade, but isn't very good at using it. Is he still alive, Cris? How did you end up with Igraine's people?"

"He's alive, I think. He traded me to Igraine in order to get access to an Angel."

The mention of that heavenly being hangs in the air like a feather, drifting down ever so slowly.

I don't want to say anymore, both because I'm worried about giving my son away, and because I don't want to talk about what happened to me in Tintagel.

El Cid refills my bloodwater.

She's giving me a pretty intense look. Does she know the truth? No, this is a different kind of look. She's intending to fuck me again.

"Keith's crew is a possibility," Q goes on. "He might have returned to the area. It might even be that Igraine found out you were lost before honoring her half of the deal. Keith might be trying to capture you again. Or, of course, it could just be some idiot who lucked out and found one of our weapons."

Or it could be my God damned son. Out there alone. Looking for something to ease his loneliness. Killing to let out his rage.

"If it's Keith and his boys," El Cid says, "it might be dangerous to scout. But if it is some idiot who picked up *my* blade, I'd like to know."

I swallow down some of the spider eggs. "Can't be," I say. "Your blade is on Soulfall, with Aiden's body."

The lie comes easy to me. I love the fuck out of Cid, and I want her to get her sword back, but I don't think I can live without the idea that my son is still out there, in some way. Selfish? Sure. A bastard move? Certainly.

But I'm on the edge here.

"Could very well be Keith, then," Neb says. "If he followed us all the way to Soulfall, he might come out searching for us."

"Any chance he'd find us?" I ask.

Q shakes his head. "It's possible. The Order has managed to compromise some of our safe houses before, but I doubt he'd even know to look."

I want to tell them the truth, to let them know that Keith isn't really out there. I really do. Self-loathing builds up in the back of my throat.

Cid frowns. "Keep your scouting close to home, Q," she says. "I think it's best if we just make sure no Minotaur is coming to call. The long-range scouting is just too dangerous. The last thing we need is an attack from the Order."

The conversation moves on, but my thoughts dwell on the Angel. On the lie I just told. On Shy.

On the empty spot inside my heart where my son used to be.

I awaken to Cid's kisses. Her fingers trace small circles on my chest. For some reason it tickles. I see the sign of the infidel, a scarification etched into her palm.

"Why aren't all things true?" she asks me.

The hell kind of question is that?

"I don't know," I tell her. "I don't think that would make sense."

She smiles. "It wouldn't, would it?"

Wait.

I look at her suspiciously. "Are you trying to teach me something?"

She draws a few more circles. "Maybe. Maybe your infidel training is more than about how to fight."

She watches her fingers as they move across me.

"Of course some things aren't true," I say. "You don't need to teach me that."

She draws an imaginary check mark on my abdomen. "But if I did need to teach you that, or let's say you had to teach someone that, how would you do so?"

I think about this. "No one's that dumb, Cid. I mean, my hand can't be open and closed at the same time. No one thinks that all things are true."

She sits up on one elbow and kisses me, her black hair spilling across my face.

"Yes, Cris. Your hand being open and closed are mutually exclusive. They can't both be true. Hell contains many universes, though. Are there going to be any where all things are true? Might you die, and someday find yourself in such a place?"

Jesus. It is way too early in the morning to be thinking about this shit.

"I think you had too much bloodwater last night," I grunt.

She kisses me and pouts. "I'm being serious, Cris."

"I don't know, Cid, you tell me."

"The statement 'all things are false' would have to be true in such a universe, right?"

I sit up and stretch. "It would have to be. But it can't be."

Her grin grows wider. "Now, could there be a

universe where everything is true except for that one sentence?"

Fuck. This is going to be a long day.

After Cid is done torturing me with ridiculous questions, we join Neb and Q in the study. El Cid leads us down the tight spiral staircase.

I fall in behind the necromancer and we follow her while Q takes the rear.

"Where we headed?" I call to her, my voice echoing louder than I expected in the tight confines.

She tosses me a friendly look over one shoulder. "The armory."

Neb and I share a glance before I feel a schoolboy grin come over my face.

As if sensing our excitement, Cid shouts back up at us, "And don't think today's going to be all shooting shit. First we've got to go over weapon maintenance. I've got to measure you for some armor. Then we've got footwork and tactics. Then we get to do the runthroughs. And if we get all that done today, *maybe* we'll fire some rounds."

My mood is picking up. Having something to *do*, that's exactly what I need right now.

"She sure knows how to talk to a fellow, doesn't she?" I say to Neb as we come out of the stairwell.

Neb seems uncomfortable. I don't think he's had a friend in years, so maybe this is too much, too fast for him.

Then he pulls it together. "She probably learned her bedside manner in the Infidel training program."

It wasn't a very funny joke, but I see something in the former Nazi I've never seen before. Neb's real smile is a precious thing, a little goofy, a little abashed, and so much friendlier than that movie star grin he'd worn before.

As we come to the armory, I glance at the circuit-breaker looking box Q pointed out earlier. It might be interesting to get trained on how to use that.

The weapons are kept behind a large steel door with one of those twisting submarine locks.

Cid is practically glowing as she comes to it. Nothing puts a spring into her step, it turns out, like munitions. She smiles as she begins spinning the lock. It twirls and twirls. I check Q's face, but he's as hard as ever. I catch his eye and grin at him, hoping to break that façade, but no luck.

He's all business today.

The armory opens, and I swear I can smell the gunpowder wafting out.

I'm not sure what I expected, but it isn't this. The chamber is more of a hall—fifty feet deep, ten feet tall, ten feet wide and it's lined with racks of weapons. Barrels of spare bullets and clips sit next to the racks. Sheets of hide are stacked up at the back of the room.

Some of the weapons are old. I recognize one as a

Mauser, maybe from World War I. Some are even older than that. A line of short swords, Roman gladii I believe, hang right next to the Mp5s. Here is a bow, and there a spear.

There are other weapons I don't even recognize.

"The hell is that?" I ask, pointing to a gun that looks like it was from a Schwarzenegger flick.

"Launches infidel fire," Q says. "Very dangerous."

"And that one?" I point at a weapon with what looks like a compressed air tank attached to one side.

"Endothermic weapon," Cid says. "Hell isn't like Earth. There's a chemical cascade you can cause which absorbs a ridiculous amount of heat. There's no ammo for it here, and they're very rare, but you're looking at what is perhaps one of the most powerful weapons in Hell."

I move up to it. The thing seems unwieldy. I bet it would be far easier to use if it were mounted on something.

"How powerful?" I ask.

Q chuckles. "More than a few infidels have frozen off their fingers just from firing the thing."

El Cid draws me away from the weapon. "Remember the lake around Portsmouth?"

I nod.

"With that, you could have frozen its surface solid and then skated across."

Neb whistles. "And the ammunition? Where can

we get some?"

"I honestly don't know," Cid says. "It's harder to make than infidel fire. Much, much harder."

She walks to the back where the hanging sheets of leather are. "Come here, boys," she says. "Let's get you measured. We'd rather make your armor out of wightskin, but in a pinch, Icanitzu skin will have to do."

I get the horrific image of wearing my son.

Q pats my shoulder. "And you thought the Eden chamber was nice."

El Cid measures us quickly and professionally. It reminds me so much of the old world that I feel a tightness in my gut.

The only time I can remember being measured for anything was for a tux at my senior prom. Earth has never seemed so far away as it does now, here in the one place in Hell that might have some similarity to it.

Cid turns to Q. "Get them trained on weapon cleaning. I'll get the armor started."

I know how to clean weapons, it was one of the first things I'd learned after escaping the City of Blood and Stone, so I'm pretty damn sure they aren't going to teach me anything. Hell, Ares had shown me how to do it himself.

Neb looks equally non-plussed. Sure, weapons had changed a bit since his training in World War II, but this could almost be considered insulting.

Q pulls down a Mp5. "Now gentleman, this is

going to be just like cleaning a normal Mp5 with one exception."

My ears perk up. Neb leans forward.

The weapon comes apart in Q's long fingers. "On Earth, you're bound by Newton," he says. "You shoot a bullet forward, there is an equal and opposite force coming back toward your ass. This can be a serious issue if you're trying to shoot through something as tough as elephant hide. In Hell, we have a few more alternatives." He pulls out the firing pin and points into the weapon. "What happens when you shoot a bullet at an Icanitzu?"

"Jack shit," I answer.

He nods. "Right, the bullet's momentum disappears. That energy is just gone. Now, there are ways Hell gets it back, but the real question you should ask is this. What would happen if an Icanitzu fired a gun?"

Shit. They'd be fucking unstoppable with a gun.

Perhaps seeing my fear, Q raises a hand. "Fortunately, they have difficulty grabbing Earth stuff. That's why clothes are always sliding around weirdly on wights and whatnot. But let's say one managed. Would they face any recoil?"

Neb mutters something in German.

"So you're saying you've got a bit of Icanitzu skin in the weapon," I say, "and that it somehow absorbs the recoil?"

Q nods. "Not all the recoil. And you have to be careful when you switch from an infidel weapon to a non-infidel one. You also have to be damn careful how you infuse the skin into the stock. I've seen an amateur jam their weapons because firing the bullet is usually what powers loading the next round. Take some of that energy away, and your next round might not find the chamber. The other issue with Icanitzu skin is that it eventually wears out. Most infidel armor uses wightskin for that reason—but it's precisely the ability of Icanitzu skin to start interacting with Earth-stuff momentum which allows us to find the right balance of absorption for your rifle. Now this kick absorption does two things for us.

"One, you can shoot normal munitions with excellent accuracy. And of course, two, you can shoot overpressure ammunition without blowing your shoulder off. As you can imagine, with the right kind of bullets, an infidel can do some serious damage to a harpy, or even a Minotaur."

For the first time since El Cid accepted me into this group, I feel like I'm finally seeing behind the curtain.

"And do we have those bullets?" Neb asks.

Q smiles. "A few. Most seem to be designed for a specific archdevil, one vulnerable to whetstone."

El Cid calls to us from where she's cutting the hide. "Maybe, but they could also be for Icanitzu. Whetstone bullets act about like old world ones do. Maybe

Archades had access to something that could forge them."

I raise my hand.

Q looks at it for a second before responding. "Yes, Cris?"

"So we get to shoot now, right?"

For a week, we spend our days training with firearms and our nights relaxing in the baths.

The first day is a look at the basics. When to put your finger on the trigger, when to leave your safety on, how to breathe. How to move in short, even steps so as to keep your torso a stable firing platform.

Day two is different. They teach Neb and I how to storm rooms. Some of it's intuitive, some of it's so counterintuitive I'm not sure if it's even the right way to do things. For instance, when I burst into a room in the point position, sometimes Cid doesn't want me to shoot the first devil I see. Depending on the layout of the chamber, I have a responsibility for a certain part of the room. If the first pretend devil isn't in my area, I'm supposed to keep on going, and the next person through will get them.

It's nuts.

Q assures me it's effective, though.

Cid sets up little racks of dyitzu skin throughout the complex, and we run through, fake shooting as we go.

We do one run with bows and arrows.

Q teaches me two different ways to approach archery.

The first is for fighting in small chambers. I draw ten or fifteen arrows and keep them in my bow hand. When I take an arrow from the bow hand, that motion becomes the draw itself. Q shows me how I can keep three arrows in my drawing hand, which is hard as hell to do, and requires precise fingering, but it does let me shoot really quickly. With these methods, the arrow runs along the far side of the bow.

The second approach is the one I remember from movies. The draw and nocking become two motions. With this method, the arrow's shaft is on the near side of the bow from your body. Q says this can be good for long range target shooting, but to me it seems to lack the physical beauty of the first approach.

Neb gets callouses from this training. Not me, I get blisters.

Mostly, however, we do the room clearing with guns. We even do two runs with live ammo. The first run got my ears ringing pretty badly, and at the end I didn't follow procedure quite right.

Cid and I had a fight about it. It just doesn't make sense for me not to shoot the first dyitzu sandbag I see. She dressed me down good, and I used her method the second time through.

"Learn everything," Q had said, "discard what is

useless."

After the baths that night, Cid made sure to fuck me especially hard.

I awaken.

Q's knocking on my door.

"What's up?" I ask.

"Different drill today. Meet us in the training room when you're up."

The training room is on the bottom floor. Stone cubbies, lined with thick dyitzu hides, run along the back wall.

Q will be coming I'm sure, but for now, it's just Cid.

She hugs me and sighs, pressing her face into my chest. She looks up. Her eyes are truly beautiful, a green so deep as to be blue. I've met kind people before, but perhaps she is the kindest. Some people can't be mean, even if they want to be. They cannot be duplicitous because they cannot bring themselves to lie. Cid is not one of those people.

She can lie. She can kill. She can be a holy horror. But she chooses not to. That makes her kindness worth so much more to me.

She steps back and takes my measure, her eyes dispassionate. Then her slender arms cross themselves under her tiny breasts.

"It's time to make a man of you," she jokes.

Q and Neb enter the room, as if on cue.

It turns out today is the start of our hand-to-hand training.

In the beginning, Neb has an advantage on me. Because of the kickboxing I did in the old world, I don't usually run into people who can outfight me, but that bastard Nazi's combat training must have been something special.

It doesn't last, though. After Cid teaches me some of that catch wrestling infidel shit, I become a monster. Even Q struggles to keep me off him. Honestly, I didn't even know fighting could be like this.

But how to fight humans is just part one. Q gets some dyitzu-hide spheres and pretends he's throwing fireballs at us. The hide isn't a perfect mimic for a fireball because gravity affects it, but it's pretty close. The infidels have made a science of evading dyitzu fire. A lot of it is similar to slipping punches and kicks, so I pick it up quickly.

At other times, Q and Cid don gloves which represent claws. This changes up the catch holds a lot and is very frustrating. Still, I'm determined to make my new skills work for me in Hell, so I struggle through.

Neb fucking hates grappling.

Secretly, I love that Neb hates it, and so I try even harder to prove that it can work.

We also learn a series of special holds for hounds.

All that is pretty glorious, but not all the training is gunpowder and rainbows.

I tell Cid that as we sit in the upstairs study.

The equation she's showing me, its numbers and letters etched into a waxen tablet, is one designed to help me figure out just how big my waterwheel would need to be to create a certain amount of force when taking into consideration a current of a certain speed.

"Really?" I ask her. "I have to learn this shit?"

"Infidels are often called to build structures like these," she answers.

I'd never seen an infidel build anything like that. "The hell for?"

"A corpse crusher, for instance." She gazes at me and perhaps reads my confusion. "They're how we clear out corpse holes, if we need to. The dead don't learn, so all you need is something that makes some noise for bait and a machine for crushing corpses."

I snicker and lean back in my chair. "Ah, a corpse crusher." The equation swims in my vision. "I don't like math."

She frowns. "Perhaps you should consider liking it. You pick it up quickly."

"It doesn't work that way, Cid," I tell her. "You can't just choose to like something."

"Oh? Why not?"

"Because . . ."

Socratic bitch.

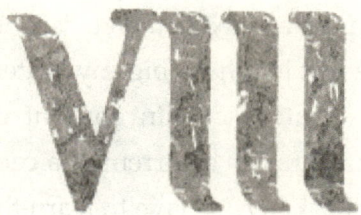

VIII

I awaken. I fuck Cid. I eat. Then I get to learning.

The Gehennic Encyclopedias are something I'd heard of before, and I've always wanted to read one. They contain the amassed knowledge of the infidels, and I'd assumed that once I'd gotten my hands on the book, damnation would finally start making some sense—which was true in a way. Only I'd expected it to read like some long lost occult tome. Instead it reads like a God damned science textbook. Worse, everything I learn, and I mean every single little damned thing, makes it clear that there are at least a dozen other things I don't know. And that's not the worst of it.

The worst is that there is so much shit even the

infidels don't know.

The pages are insanely thin, thousands of them in a single millimeter, and they're made out of some sort of clear substance that will not tear, yet bends easily. There's probably an article about how to make it somewhere in here. Because the pages are clear, they're almost impossible to read unless you put something under them. I use a white handkerchief which Cid gives me. I think I've seen it before because the "CW" embroidered in its corner is familiar. It's got a smudge of black dried blood on it, so I occasionally have to move it around under the page to read the black scrawl of the book.

I flip to "dyitzu." If there's anything in Hell I understand, it's dyitzu.

After about a page, I begin to second guess myself.

Cid is flipping through her own book.

"They don't focus with their eyes?" I ask her. "They focus with their mind?"

She turns to me, and her eyes narrow.

I realize there is no way for her to know what I'm talking about. "Dyitzu, I mean."

She grins. "Isn't that some cool shit? Let me see if I can help explain it. When did you die?"

"In the Eighties," I tell her.

"Well, if you talk to someone who died twenty or so years after you, they might be familiar with a camera which uses the same concept. A lens will take in all the light, the data will be stored, and then a computer program can focus the image at different depths. Amazing, yes?"

"Yes, amazing," I say. "Why the hell would their eyes be like that?"

Cid shrugs. "There's a surprisingly large amount of writing about that. Endymion thinks it's what we might expect an eye to look like if it were designed by a mind rather than selected for by reproductive fitness. There could still be evolutionary pre-cursors that organically select an eye like that, and we should be careful because on Earth, many people made the mistake of confusing selective designs with intelligent ones. Hell, though, seems to tell a different story. For instance, a harpy is a combination of a mammal and a bird. It also corresponds with myths which a lot of us are fairly certain human beings made up."

The idea is more horrifying than my usual thoughts about Hell.

I close the encyclopedia, confident that her handkerchief will keep my place. "You mean there's something out here manufacturing our nightmares for us?"

She gazes at the wall as if she were looking through it. "I really think so, Cris. But I don't know what or why. I think it wants us to experience something. Haven't you ever wondered why we have food to eat? Why weapons are given to us? Why we always have a chance to survive? I think there's something out there, Cris, that doesn't focus on us individually, but which wants humans to have some kind of experience in general. A terrible one, I think."

"But why?"

She shrugs. "Sadism, perhaps. But an artistic one because our pain certainly isn't maximized. Some of the Norse thought that this was just another level to hone our skills. That we would become better and better fighters as we died until we were ready to defend Valhalla. Endymion even suggested it might be some form of digestion. There could be many entities, with differing wishes, which might explain why some things are built to kill us, and others are built to save us. But we call whatever it or they are, the thing or things that made our local conditions this way, who built all the strange hallways and pillars and rivers, Hell's Architect."

I'd heard the term, certainly, but I'd never thought of it in this way.

"Doesn't anyone know what it is for sure?" I ask.

She gives me a sad smile. "That's one of the things Ares used to lament. 'No one stopped us on our way down to tell us what was going on.'"

I think about this for a moment. "Couldn't the Architect be Satan?"

She cocks her head to one side. "Maybe, but how does that make sense?"

She exasperates me sometimes. "This is Hell, Cid. Everyone calls it that. People on Earth thought there was an afterlife. They said that God made Hell. Maybe they got some of the details wrong, but it sure feels like they were pretty close to the mark. How could it not make sense?"

"So you're telling me you'd look into the eyes of a full on Greek mythos harpy, and suddenly you're a believer in Yahweh?"

There is more of the gunpowder and rainbows training too. They teach me all kinds of things. How to shoot a man while surrendering a weapon — which seems mighty unethical. How to wield a knife. How to use the outside of my arm as a shield against a slashing blade — something I hope I never do.

We take a two-day crash course on how to climb in the Eden chamber. We use braided sinfruit vines as rope. The carabiners we put into the wall seem ridiculous, as the highest we can get is about thirty feet. Nonetheless, Q gets us in the habit of securing and communicating before we make any further progress.

There are many varying strategies on how to fight Hell's creatures, I soon find. They teach me a circular dance you can use with other infidels to defeat a single powerful opponent by attacking from all sides. They teach me that certain creatures, like harpies, are almost immune to bullets because of their skin, but that if you pierce their hide, your weapons can pulp their insides.

They show me how to use the right tools to take apart bullets and use their shells to fire hellstone instead. But at the end of the day, when we're done fighting and shooting and climbing and eating and bathing, I always find myself back in the study.

Cid shifts on her chair, throwing one leg over an upholstered arm, sitting spread eagle like a man might. "You haven't exercised the part of your brain that learns academically in years, but it's worth the mental sit-ups. Believe me."

I grunt and shake my head.

"It can't be harder than killing that dyitzu on the cliffs of the Erebus," she says. "You were dehydrated. Your ankle was fucked up. The will that must have taken . . ."

"I didn't . . ." I begin, looking up at her.

She's studying me intently. But there was a dead dyitzu near the cliffs of the Erebus, because Aiden had killed it to feed me.

Cid is fucking smart as Hell, and I'm pretty sure her suspicious mind is on to something.

I shake my head. "I don't think I was really conscious when that happened, Cid. It was like killing something in a fever dream."

She nods, perhaps accepting my story. "You've recovered fast, too. I mean, you're still good and sorely mind-fucked, don't get me wrong. Had you fallen to the stilling, I would have understood—but you *healed* quickly, Cris. Some part of you hasn't given up. Sometimes I thought your son was a crutch you leaned on, and that you needed to save him more than he even needed saving. That you used him for the motivation you needed to face Hell. I guess I was mistaken."

No, Cid. No you weren't.

I return my gaze to the waxen tablet I've been etching math on and try to think. If the wheel has a three foot radius, then the . . . fuck, now I really can't focus.

Have I really been using my son? I had thought that having a child gave me different priorities. I had thought that for the first time in my existence I had actually been living with someone else's priorities in front of my own—but what if Cid is right? What if I needed to put him first because I wasn't emotionally strong enough to face a universe which wants to kill me? What if my love for him really is selfish?

I remember his cold black eyes, staring at me with a kind of hatred a normal iris simply could not hold.

And I loved him anyway. Was I loving him for himself, or was I loving him for me?

"Are you okay, Cris?" Cid asks.

I don't feel good at all now.

"No," I tell her. "No, Cid. I'm not okay. I'm not sure I'm going to be okay."

Cid is gentle tonight.

I awaken in Cid's arms, my cheek on her chest. I can hear the soothing rhythm of her heartbeat reverberating evenly in my ear. My soul is aching from the loss of my son. My entire body is sore from the terrible things the infidels did to me yesterday in fight training—that and the wonderful things Cid did to me in the night.

Sometimes she can be as dominant as Fellmen.

I remember his body jerking as he died. Din had stabbed him. My hands are shaking again.

I push the memories down and try to focus on something else.

The fight training has been helpful. I've been doing pretty good. Well, at least I can kick Neb's ass.

It'll take me a while before I can beat Q, though I've been giving him a good run for his money.

Her hands find my back and gently squeeze one aching trapezius. Hard like iron, her tiny fingers knead their way into my muscle. My body relaxes at her touch. It knows her and trusts her far more than my mind does.

I think my body is probably a good judge of character.

She whispers to me, shaking me from my reverie, "Someday you'll face a reckoning, my lover—one more potent than that Christian apocalypse you sometimes believe in." She's staring up toward the ceiling, her expression troubled as if she's fighting with her own inner demons. "There will come a time, after your learning and your fighting, when you will meet the Infidel. He will see you and know that you've been trained by his people. He will know that you are one of his. He will know your abilities, your worthiness, your heart and your mind. It's best to be at peace with yourself and your character when that day comes. I cannot describe to you what it would be like to face his rejection—or to have to reject yourself in his presence."

"You suck at pillow talk, baby," I say.

"Sweetheart, I'm trying to save you from something."

I turn and look at her exquisitely beautiful face. "I'm not afraid."

She frowns. "Nor was I. I hadn't been in Hell long enough to really know who he was when I first met him—I could tell, in a way, but I just didn't *know*. But, there was a time, later, when I feared I'd become a leader out of pride, and I was afraid he'd see that and judge me for it."

I imagine the meeting, me and that man, that demigod whose statue and shadow I've seen, his piercing eyes digging into my soul—laying bare the love I hold for my son. Would that love prove selfish? Would it matter? I feel sick to my stomach, and I push the thoughts away.

I remember Nebuchadnezzar saying the Infidel had fucked Cid. I feel a pang of jealousy building up in my stomach.

"You and the Infidel, Neb thought you'd slept together," I say.

Her green eyes regard me coolly. "I told you I love you in the way that *I* love people. You understand? I don't love you the way *you* love."

The jealousy builds up, sitting in the base of my throat like heartburn. "The hell is that supposed to mean?"

"You don't own me, Cris."

"Did he?" I ask. "Did he fuck you? Does he own you?"

She pushes herself up, sitting on her knees like a Japanese warrior. "When we brought you here, you were dying inside. Q was worried about the stilling —"

"Answer my question, Cid." I hear my anger boiling in my voice.

She doesn't respond to me at all. "You pulled through. Me fucking you, Cris, did that help you?"

"Not one damn bit," I spit at her.

Of course it didn't, right? I think back to that moment, the first time. I remember the darkness I was in. The darkness I'm in now. The hopelessness.

I feel the damnation that contaminates my soul, and I remember how deeply it had crept into my mind. It's still back there, with the memories of Fellman and Melvin, waiting like a tide to come forth and sweep my sanity away.

She cocks her head to one side.

"No, you're right," I say, lowering my head. "You didn't just help me. You saved me."

She shrugs. "Maybe. I think you would have made it through anyway. You're very tough, Cris, in body, mind and spirit. But you know what it's like to be almost down. You know what it's like to need to be saved."

"And the Infidel?" I ask.

"He saved me."

I swallow down the bile of jealousy. "And did he, did he love you in the way that infidels do?"

She nods.

"I don't want this, Cid," I tell her. "I don't want

that kind of love. I want real love. I want the patient, kind love."

She reaches out with a delicate looking hand and touches the beard I've grown. "Love is patient, love is kind. It does not envy, it does not boast, it is not proud. It does not dishonor others, it is not self-seeking, it is not easily angered, it keeps no record of wrongs. Love does not delight in evil but rejoices with truth. It always protects, always trusts, always hopes, always perseveres."

"Yes, I say. That kind of love. The kind between a man and a wife. The kind that was on Earth."

She stands up, her head tilted down toward me. "You've never met a woman like me, Cris. When you meet other infidels, though, other women worth a shit, you'll find that I'm not as special as you think. Meet a few of them before you decide."

I shake my head. "There's no one like you, Cid. No one."

She smiles. "Rise, Cris. I have to make you into something. I have to turn your blood into lava and your body into whetstone. I have to turn your mind into a raging current of lightning, your will into an avalanche, your soul into a wellspring. And then, when you have learned to despise Hell, when you know her weaknesses, when you know how to break her, then I have to unleash you.

"On that day, Cris, we'll speak of silly little things

like patient love."

I meet Q in the study.

He looks at me and runs a hand across his clean-shaven face. Then he produces a folded razor from his pocket and tosses it to me.

I catch it in my right hand. The handle is made of some kind of bone. I flip out the blade and examine it. It could be old world, but with the infidels, it's impossible to know.

"What's up with this?" I ask.

"There were a few in the armory."

"Thanks," I say.

Q smiles. "You're getting scruffy. That's a bad look for you anyway. And as an infidel, we need you well groomed."

I'd always wondered about that. "Why?"

Q raises an eyebrow.

"Why do we bother looking nice?" I clarify.

"A few reasons. Personal upkeep is an important thing. There's no shame in letting yourself go if there's no time to groom, but it's a good habit. Grounding. Lets the universe know it hasn't won. But maybe there's a more pragmatic reason as well."

"Oh?"

He gives me a rueful smile. "We have enough of a public relations problem as it is, don't you think? You've heard how the people around Maylay Beighlay feel about us. I can't see how us being ugly would help any of that."

Infidel humor sometimes escapes me.

"You can shave in the john," Q says.

I shrug. "Maybe I like the beard?"

He laughs. "Do you? Cid doesn't. She's been complaining about it."

"Point taken."

I turn to walk back down the hallway.

"Wait," Q says.

I look back at him.

"Are you okay? We need to set up this false trail, and I need help to do it. Cid's busy making you and Neb's armor right now. I'd take you normally . . ."

Am I okay? I think on this, and suddenly I see my son's black eyes staring up at me from the depths of my memory.

"And we'll save people?" he had asked.

What the hell had he meant by that?

I stretch my sore arms. "Yeah, man. I mean, I'm not okay. I'm all fucked up. But this, this Hell thing, that I can do."

"Shave quickly," he says, unconvinced. "Use some lather. I don't want a hound picking up the scent of your blood. Now we can't go far because Keith might be out there, but a little motion will do you some good, I think."

My heart sinks. It's not Keith out there. It's my son.

If Q sees him . . .

But maybe it's better if I'm out there with him.

For a moment I wonder what things would have been like if they hadn't saved me. If Shy and I had found Aiden.

I make my way to the bathroom and open the door. The lightstone which illuminates my face is warm. I look at myself in the mirror. My eyes are dead.

With an unsteady hand, I raise the razor.

I watch the blade shake in the mirror.

How the hell am I supposed to shave like this?

XI

Hell is suddenly unfamiliar. The cruel, grey stones which pass under my feet have been worked over by the Architect, but the dark ceilings above are jagged, natural, and hateful. I search inside myself for the confidence I used to feel when passing through Hell's halls, but it's gone. Even my Old Lady feels unfamiliar in my hands.

I've lost faith in myself.

It's because I've been beaten. I fought Hell with everything I had, everything the infidels had, and Hell still took my boy away. Then it took my dignity.

That's when Hell gets you. It breaks you first, preparing you for the next level of damnation, and then it kills you.

I'm a dead man walking.

The heel of my shoe scuffs the stone floor, and Q turns to me quickly.

It's happening already. I'm usually quieter than this. What if it's a careless slip up like that which alerts my son to our presence, and then he comes to find us and Q sees him and Q will shoot him because —

Stop, Cris. Focus.

I look to the two dark entrances to this corridor. There could be something out there other than Aiden which could have heard my misstep.

My breathing seems louder somehow.

Q, infidel quiet, begins moving again, motioning me forward.

Jesus Christ, I'm going to get us killed out here.

As softly as I can, I follow.

He stops in the next room and points up to a vein of muted emerald green skystone which flows through the dark cave rock. He means we're following the vein.

I nod to let him know I've caught on.

He shakes his head and points again.

I take another look at the ceiling. There's a bit of variation in the color. In places the emerald hue is a little lighter, but I have no idea what he's pointing at.

I meet his eyes and shrug my shoulders, holding my hands out to signal that I don't understand.

Q doesn't seem perturbed.

He won't die. Hell hasn't broken him yet.

Unless he cares about me as much as I care about him. Then my death might make him ripe for Hell.

I follow my infidel friend through the next couple of rooms. He points again to the ceiling.

It's the same emerald skystone.

Fuck, I'm so lost.

It's got that same hue variation, though. In places, it almost seems yellow.

Oh shit. It's a cross-vein. I knew it could happen, but I'd never noticed something as subtle as a series of skystone veins running through skystone before.

As we move on I begin to see it more clearly. How could I have been so fucking stupid to have missed this? The emerald skystone is running in one direction, following the passages of the naturally roofed caverns. But the more yellow skystone veins are doing something else. They're traveling at maybe a fifteen degree angle away from the main vein.

Now I can see it in the floor stones as well.

Hell has synergies like this. If you follow a vein, the passages just open up for you. Dead ends are rarer, and you seldom travel in circles. I feel it now, this forward momentum caused by moving with the grain of Hell.

How had I missed this when Q first pointed it out to me?

And how often had I missed this before?

Were there such subtle cross veins along that river

where Myla, Aiden and I had lived for so long? And what a useful tool to use to escape an enemy. You get better speed following a vein in Hell, true, but you are easier to track. Every once in a while, it's like all the paths in a vein converge into a single chamber, and there would be your enemy.

If you knew about one of these cross-veins though, you could still get great speed, but it'd be damn hard to cut you off.

Our next room is a much larger cavern, and I see the true color of the skystone we'd been following. It's a brilliant, almost neon orange. Its light isn't enough to do much more than highlight the edges of the dark stones and glint off the worked floor, but where it shoots along the ceiling like frozen lightning, its color is intense.

A natural structure of stone breaks through the even grey bricks and rises, forming a bridge to meet a passage high on the cavern's wall.

Q holds up one finger and then points to the bridge.

He steps upon the strange rock formation, and then holds up a hand, signaling me to stop.

Oh, I get it. Only one person on the bridge at a time.

As graceful as only an infidel can be, he moves quickly along the bridge. It's only a yard wide at its narrowest, and it gets to be about twenty feet tall, so I'm not too keen on following him.

Shit, I should be checking exits. Q's vulnerable.

I'm fucking this up pretty bad.

I shoulder the Old Lady and peer into the dark, cavernous exits. Then I look back to Q, who's made it to the passage above. He's unslung his M-16 and is ready to take up the watch. I slide the Old Lady back into my pack and step on the stone bridge. Detritus strewn along the top of the span crunches a little under my feet.

It seems impossible to move up quietly, so I'm not sure how Q managed it. I do my best. I stay low as I climb, fearing the fall. My foot slips noisily and I catch myself on the rock.

Pebbles rattle on the floor.

Finally I meet Q. He's not looking at me, thank God, because I feel damn guilty for how shitty a companion I'm being right now.

The orange skystone vein is clearer and easier to see now that we've left the emerald. I follow, a clumsy child in Q's wake.

Q's leaving this false trail for Keith, but Keith isn't the one who's following us.

Should I do something, make some change, leave some sort of signal so Aiden knows to avoid this?

A nearly colorless type of crystal is getting pretty common in the cavern walls. It glints with the orange of the skystone, shining at me in some places like a giant faceted insect eye. In other places the crystal is so clear I can see right through it to the rock walls it's embedded in. Here and there, the crystal acts like a window, providing glimpses into the chambers beyond.

I don't dare leave Aiden any kind of sign. What could I hope to leave behind that Q wouldn't detect?

And what if Aiden is already in these tunnels, searching for us? I guess he'll just pass us by. He'll follow whatever route Q leaves for him, and he'll be gone forever. Lost to me. Alone in the infinite labyrinth.

I'm struck suddenly that there's no way out of Hell—not even death. You can only go deeper.

I just want to run back to the Eden room. Who cares if bliss can't last? Let the Minotaurs come. Let them all come and tear me limb from limb. At least I'll have a few moments of peace. Let Aiden find my dead body.

That has to be worth something.

That has to be worth something.

That has to be—

My legs are shaking—my whole *body* is shaking.

"I can't," I say.

Q pauses, not turning around.

"Q, I have to go back."

He walks gingerly into the next room.

"Don't leave me here!" I shout, and my voice echoes in the cold silence of Hell.

I'm so fucking stupid. I've got to get back. I hold up the Old Lady and look desperately toward the exits of the room. My aim is so shit right now. Sweat is pouring down the side of my face.

"Easy," Q says.

But I can't be easy. And I can't tell him why. And—

"Easy," he repeats, his voice closer. "There are more devils in your mind, Cris, than in the wilds around us. I'm going to show you something. Follow me."

I take some deep breaths. Q's not waiting around, so I jog a few steps to catch up and follow him into the next room.

It's very dim with only a small portion of the orange skystone vein showing through the ceiling. The chamber's right wall is almost completely made of crystal. The orange light of the vein reflects off its glasslike surface. Caught up in it are tiny pieces of hellstone gravel which hang there, as if floating, trapped in the transparent substance.

On the far side of that crystal are a dozen or so corpses.

I level the Old Lady.

They spot us and move, staggering, stumbling, heaving and lurching toward the clear wall. Q raises one hand and lets his fingertips touch lightly against the crystal.

He motions for me to come over to him. Then he points through the glass, first at one side of the room. Then the other. Q turns around and starts to head out the way we entered. I move to follow, but he stops me with an open hand, pointing again toward the corpses.

Oh, damn. I have to stay here and keep them occupied.

I'm the bait.

I walk up to the glasslike wall.

The corpses aren't the danger. I need to watch the two exits to this room.

Q leaves, and I put my back to the crystal.

I can hear the undead fingers as they scrape and scrape and scrape.

Don't look at them, Cris, just focus on the exits.

One room, then the other.

The scratching continues.

One room, then the other.

How long will I be here? Fifteen minutes? An hour? Five hours?

A day?

What if I see some evidence of Aiden? Could he have come through here?

One room, then the other.

If only their clawing was rhythmic, then I could start to ignore it. The corpses, however, are almost human in their desperation to get at me.

I need to tell my friends what's going on. I have to tell Cid. I have to tell Q. I can explain to them that Aiden wanted me to help people. I can explain that Aiden is different from other wights. And who's to say he can't overcome this?

One room, then the other.

I can either tell them, or lose my son forever.

Forever.

But we'll both be in one of these Hells, Gehenna or Sheol or whatever comes after that, forever. Aren't we destined to meet again?

And then I'm reminded of the different universes El Cid had spoken of. If we're in the wrong kind of universe, I'll never see him again, no matter how long we stay.

Please, God, let Hell not be like that.

Or if it takes too long, will we even remember each other?

After a billion lifetimes and a billion deaths, will we even recognize the strange tortured souls we've become? Or the strange worlds we inhabit? Will we be pitted against each other without us ever knowing the nature of our true relationship? Has that happened to us already?

One room, then the other.

The scratching stops for a second.

Oh Hell.

I turn on my heel.

The undead are there, looking at me.

A smaller one than the rest has made its way to the crystal wall.

My heart leaps . . .

But it's not my son.

The scratching continues. The young corpse only has one eye, the other lost to rot. The wound which killed him was in his torso. Jagged ribs and an exposed lung peek out through the tear in his shirt.

Then I see movement in the rear of the corpses' chamber.

It's Q, slinking his way across the room. He'll return soon.

I turn my back to him and the dead.

One room, then the other.

One room, then the other.

One room, then the other.

That has to be worth something.

That has to be worth something.

That has to be worth something.

So what is it, then? Do I tell them and hope they will do the wrong thing? Do I let my son wander away forever?

But he's smart. And he'll be looking for me, probably around Maylay Beighlay because that's where he had a family last.

Only, he'll have no idea how to get there. And nor do I, unless I can find the Northern Lethe.

I can't do it.

I can't tell them.

I can't kill my own son.

That has to be worth something.

So that means I'm going to have to make a choice.

Her sensual voice whispers in my ear. "I like you better shaved."

Her fingertips run down the stubble on my cheeks. Then she traces circles along my chest again, and I remember. . .

I feel dead inside. Used. Cid enjoyed it, but I didn't, and it reminded me of Melvin and Fellman's lust. How quickly the rush of being freed from Igraine's people had faded.

Then something shifts inside me. An ugly fire leaps up in my soul, catching in my brain. I feel trapped, resting in the crook of her shoulder again—as if she were the man.

Maybe she is.

The secret of my son is destroying me, tearing me up inside. The longer we stay by the Erebus, the more likely Q will be to see him. Why can't we just leave? Why do I have to be trapped in this damn safe house. If we could go. If we could get far far far far away from here.

"I'm dying, Cid," I whisper.

She knows I'm telling the truth, I see it in her half-lidded eyes. Her breath tickles my neck, and it annoys me.

Q's laid his false trail. Sooner or later Aiden's going to stumble upon it. Follow it. Head into oblivion. I shouldn't be here. I have to get out, and not just to get away. I should be with Aiden.

He could be in danger.

I've got to get out there. I've got to find him.

My breathing quickens, as if I'm sprinting, and sweat begins seeping from my pores.

Her eyes narrow. "I'm worried about you."

The fire stirs further. I try to quench it, but all this shit, all the rapes and the loss, it's breaking free.

A frown crosses her face for a moment. "We searched for you along the Erebus for three days before we found where you landed, Cris, dodging dyitzu every step of the way. I was so worried for you. Then we had to track you, and there was that damn chamber with a thousand exits . . . Q wouldn't let us leave."

Oh God.

Of course I'm going crazy. If they'd left me, I'd still be with Domina. She'd have listened to me about Aiden. A tame wight would have been all I needed to get myself in her good graces. God damn it. If Cid just hadn't cared so much. If Q hadn't been such a damned loyal friend. *That's* why.

If they weren't such fucking moral monsters, I'd be with my son.

Why can't they have a heart for a wight?

Why can't they see that passion sometimes has to override what is right?

Why can't they see that we have to help him?

"Why couldn't you have just left me?" I shout.

El Cid jerks back. I've both hurt her and confused her. She sits on her knees.

"Because we love you, Cris."

This is the moment. I have to choose between them and my son, and my son has to come first.

I jump to my feet.

"Like infidels love, right?"

She nods.

Domina had owned slaves, but she didn't want to. She would have loved me for real. I know that now. It wouldn't have been this soulless, empty shit Cid calls love. She and I could have found Aiden, and under Igraine we could have raised him together.

Yes, I'd be tortured. Yes, it would be the worst

possible fate for me—but I'm a *father*. If that's what it takes for me to give my son what he needs, that's what I'll accept.

I bend down to her. "Your love is useless. It's bullshit. You've got an empty heart, Cid. You pretend to care, but you can't feel anything. The Infidel has burnt you out inside."

Her eyes are sorrowful.

But she doesn't care. Not really. When people really care, they act on their emotions. She doesn't. She's a stone fucking bitch.

"You use people, Cid!" I screech. "You said I did that, but I'm nothing like you. Nothing. You have it in your head that you need to be a leader. You're so prideful. Well if you'd let someone else lead, Aiden would be alive. You're going to get us killed, Cid. Killed with your stupid pride."

She leans back and comes slowly to her feet. In the smoothness of that motion, I'm reminded of how much a killer this girl is.

Her head cocks to one side, her visage looking as if the Infidel himself had sculpted her stoic features. "I divulged that insecurity to you in confidence, Cris. You're not to use it to hurt me." She advances on me. "Get ready. We're doing more room clearing training today."

She bends over, picks up the bundle of her clothes, and passes me by.

No time for that. I've got to get out of here. I've got to find Aiden.

"No," I say.

She opens the door, and then, slowly, looks over her shoulder at me. "Then you can explain to Q why you are disobeying me."

I want to kill her. "I'm leaving, Cid. I don't need you."

She steps out, pausing in the hallway. "Q," she says, apparently seeing him in the study. "Something's wrong. Get a weapon and guard Cris' door. He's not to leave."

I rush to the door, but stop cold when she produces a pistol from her bundle of clothes and points it at my face.

"You can't do this!" I shout. "You're an infidel. I don't have to stay with you. You don't take slaves."

She closes the door behind her. I hear the lock click.

Fuck.

I bang my fist against the door. Then I kick it.

I won't be kept from Aiden, and I know they won't shoot me when I break through. I'm getting outside this damn complex, and I'm finding my son.

I take a few steps back and ram my shoulder into the door.

Damn infidel construction. It doesn't budge. It's like Cid's heart. Unyielding. Perfectly built to prevent bad people like myself from visiting ruin on others.

Neb. Neb's on my side. He'll help me.

"Nebuchadnezzar!" I shout. "Neb!"

I slam into the door again, and again, and again. "Neb!"

"He's in the garden room." I hear Q's voice from the other side of the heavy door.

"Let me out, Q." I can hear the tears and frustration in my voice.

There's a moment of silence.

"Q!"

"Cris. What's going on? Tell me what's wrong."

"Q!"

"Please tell me, Cris. You know I love you. You know I'd die for you. I know you'd die for me. Just tell me."

He'll kill Aiden. "Q! Please, Q. Just trust me. Just let me out. I can't say. I can't, but you have to trust me."

"You've been through a lot, Cris," Q says. "Your son's gone, you've been raped. It's going to hurt. There's no shame in it hurting."

I slam into the door again, and the uselessness of it doesn't matter. I have nothing else. No Myla. No Aiden.

So I beat myself against the door. It's like a metaphor for my existence. The door is bound to win. No amount of will or strength from me will ever break it. I will break before it does. Only, I have no choice. Breaking is all I can do.

"Q!"

But he can't break either. He's an infidel. They're not made like normal people. Or they had been, before the Infidel got to them.

"Q!" I shout as I barrel into the door again.

"Q!"

From where I lay on the ground, I can see the light spilling in from the hallway beyond as the door slowly opens. El Cid's shadow runs across the stone floor.

I'm not sure if I knocked myself unconscious or if I just passed out from exhaustion.

I cannot make out her face against the light.

She's still for a moment. "Get up, Cris."

I don't have to do what she says.

I roll over.

"Get up, Cris," she repeats. "Get up and come see your son."

Cid stops me at the door where they're keeping Aiden.

"He hadn't yet picked up our false trail," she says. "Q thinks your boy changed himself into a wight on Soulfall, rather than into a human."

She points to the room at the end of the hall. "He was being followed by one of Keith's men. My guess is that they were trailing him in hopes he'd lead them to us. That worked, but I captured them both cleanly, so we might be safe."

But I don't care about Keith or his boys. I nod toward my son's door.

Cid opens it.

This time it's my shadow which stretches out into

the dark room.

My son is seated in the blackness, cross-legged, in the back corner of the small stone chamber. The light makes it just far enough to illuminate one of his bare feet. I guess he's lost his shoes.

El Cid says something else, but I can't hear her.

I watch her shadow cross my own as she leaves.

Slowly, step by step, I enter the room.

My son's black eyes catch the light from the door as he looks up.

He stands.

I feel pressure building up inside me. It's the pain of losing him. The joy stolen at that moment on Soulfall when I thought he was saved. The anxiety of lying to my friends. The agony of the Eden chamber.

"You are evil, Father," he says, standing up to face me. "You know I'm on the winning side. You know that—"

"You found me," I say, the words tumbling from my lips.

He steps back against the wall.

My will breaks and I run to him, catching him up in my arms, tears spilling down my cheeks.

His body is so cold, and heavier than it ought to be. He doesn't smell like a person. I sense the faint tang of wightdust in the back of my throat as if even the slightest hint of it could awaken the dose he'd given me before.

"I love you, Aiden," I breathe. "I love you so much. I love you past death. Past undeath. Past anything. I'm sorry I let your mother take you. I'm sorry I let you down. I'm sorry for everything."

"Let go of me," he says, his voice cracking. "You're evil."

But he can't fool me. He needs me as much as I need him.

I feel his tears soaking into the shoulder of my shirt. And then, slowly, I feel his arms hug me back. His cold body shakes with his sobs.

Wights can cry. I know that now—just like infidels can.

I let go and step back.

His soul is warped, his eyes are black, but that fear—that pain a child has upon losing their parent, he has that. He's a monster, sure, but monsters can be alone. Monsters can be scared. Monsters can be just as tortured by this Hell as the rest of us. He wasn't supposed to be alone. His Archdevil-cum-father should be teaching him now. His mother should be guiding him. Other wights should be mentoring him.

But he has none of that. All he has is me.

Just me.

Maybe I'm not such a bad role model for a devil child. I've been a monster. I'd be a monster again to help him.

"Don't let them back in," Aiden says. "Please."

He means Q and Cid. Christ, what had they done to him?

"Did they hurt you?" I ask.

He regains a bit of his composure. "Q. He, he made me say things. He knows my mind. He . . . he's like Xyn."

I'm not sure if I'd heard that name before.

"Xyn? Who's Xyn?"

Aiden's eyes glint in the light. "My father. My other father. The one you killed. Q can read minds."

Aiden had no doubt fallen for the bullshit Xyn had been slinging. The Archdevil had claimed psychic abilities. When confronted with a well-trained infidel, that might be the best conclusion a young boy's mind could draw—if he believed in such things.

Oh shit. Q understands him. Q can know if he was sincere about wanting to help people.

"You still want to help us?" I ask.

He nods. "Yes. I want to help you resist Hell."

If he isn't lying . . . then . . .

I feel my heart beating in my chest. Maybe, just maybe, some part of my son has survived!

But I feel something else too. I've played this game with Hell before. This kind of good luck, well, it usually happens right before everything rots out from underneath you.

Like on Soulfall, when my son could have been saved.

I've got to talk to Q.

I burst out into the hallway.

Cid is there.

"Where's Q?" I demand.

She wants to talk to me, I can tell.

She jabs a thumb over one shoulder. "Collecting knowledge fruit in the garden. He wants to give Keith's man time to stew."

Keith's man? I don't have time to think about that. The garden — Eden chamber.

I rush by her, but pause before I enter the study. "Why?" I ask her, not turning around. "Why didn't you kill him?"

"Look at me, Cris."

I do.

She closes Aiden's door, locking it. She walks up to me. Her tiny hands reach up and pull me down to her. Then she pushes up with her toes and kisses me. Her tongue traces tiny circles in my mouth.

She's not mad at me? How?

For a moment she stops, and I can feel her breath on my wet lips. "Tell me you love me, Cris."

"I love you."

"Tell me you love me with the patient love."

"I do. Cid. I love you with all my heart."

"I didn't kill him because I knew you wouldn't want me to."

I pull back from her. "But you're an infidel."

Her head is tilted back a little to look up at me. "And so are you, Cris."

But her code—she's a paladin, like Myla used to call me. I put her in this position. I made her compromise herself.

"I'm sorry," I say.

She gives me a sad smile. "You broke our trust, Cris. It's a hard thing to regain."

"I'm sorry for that too, but I meant I'm sorry for making you break your code."

Her eyes narrow. "You think sparing Aiden was immoral?"

Wasn't it? Won't he kill now? Well, I suppose he can't while we've got him locked up.

"He says he wants to help people," I tell her.

She looks back over her shoulder toward his door. "He does."

"So you don't think it's immoral to spare him?"

Her green eyes return to me. "Cris, being an infidel means you have to weigh the unpleasant choices. It means you must weigh them carefully, to not shy away from them, to choose them if you need to. But it does *not* mean you always have to take that path."

Had I lied for nothing?

"I . . ."

"You surround yourself with white lies, Cris. All people do, even infidels can at times. Some of those lies are helping you tell the black ones, though. Aiden had talked to you. You *knew* he was alive. You can never tell me a black lie again, Cris. Do you understand?"

I just fucked everything. El Cid hadn't given up. Q hadn't given up. They're infidels. They *never* give up.

"How can you trust me?" I ask. "Even if I promise I . . ."

Her head cocks to one side. "I can trust you because I know you, Cris. I know you are going to say yes. I know you're going to mean it, to try to keep it, but that you can't. And I know you're going to try as hard as you can to become the kind of man who can keep that promise."

These infidels seem so cold. You're drawn to them for their strength. But I'd misjudged them. I'd misjudged her. As powerful as I thought she was, it's still quite possible that I've never underestimated someone quite so much. The most important thing about them was that they loved. Not the patient romantic or teenage-style-all-consuming love I'd learned about in the old world, but a different kind, a universal kind. El Cid loves all people. From Keith, to me, to the grey babies she'd been forced to slaughter on Soulfall.

It's so clear to me now. How had I thought any differently?

She loves us all.

Not even Jesus had that kind of love. He sent

people to Hell. If Cid ruled the universe, no one would be damned.

She is more merciful than Jesus. More merciful than God.

One of her small hands reaches out to me, her fingers touching my shirt. "I've been where you are." She draws some of the circles there that she had when we'd lain together in my room. "Go to Q," she says. "Ask him what you need to ask. Return to me, my lover, when you can. I think you forget sometimes that my heart is yours in a very real way. Not *only* yours, but yours nonetheless."

I'd hurt her. I'd hurt her badly.

But like she said, I'd make it up to her. She'll turn me into an infidel and then I'll make it up to her a thousandfold.

Right now I need to get to Q. I need to learn what's wrong—or what's right, rather—with my son.

I head for the garden.

The gentle rush of the waterfall calms my beating heart. The slight humidity, the warm lighting, the temperate air, it gives me a pleasant emotional detachment I have not felt in some time.

Q is midway up the wall on the far side of the chamber, a bag of fruit over one shoulder. I see Q's sword resting against the rock, and it makes me smile. Q deserved to get that back. He climbs down the vines, a single sinfruit escaping from his bag and tumbling across the grass. I stroll toward him, taking in the air, crossing the bridge, meeting him at the bench beneath a hungerleaf tree in a field of green devilwheat shoots.

He takes a seat.

I join him.

Mist rises from where the waterfall meets the pond, hovering in the air, settling across the nearby hungerleaves. Tiny droplets form there, swelling, growing, becoming heavy and ripe, glinting in the light of the skystone before falling into the pond below. In other places along the rock wall, the drops are more fluid, dripping like a constant rain.

God it's beautiful.

I lean forward and put my elbows on my knees.

Q is sitting with perfect infidel posture.

"My son claims he wants to help people resist Hell," I say, hearing the desperate hope in my words, "is that true?"

Because I'm leaning forward, I have to look over my shoulder to see his face.

It's as stoic as ever.

"It is true," he says.

My heart picks up again, but I struggle to stay calm, to feel that detachment the chamber afforded me only a moment ago.

I take in a deep breath, and let it out slowly. "Does that mean we don't have to kill him?"

"Aiden's idea is unstable," Q says. "It will not last."

My heart sinks. I knew it. I fucking knew it. Hell is this way. It drops you lower and lower and lower, and just when you find one single thing to fucking salvage out of all the bullshit, just when you reach out to grab it, it crumbles away and you sink even farther.

Another breath. "How do you know? Why?"

Q leans forward as well. He reaches out with one of his long arms and plucks a single strand of devilwheat. He puts it between his teeth. It reminds me of a painting from the old world. Like me, he puts his elbows on his knees. With one of his hands, he rubs his shaved scalp.

"Wights are an ingenious creation," Q says. "They maintain individuality. They have different abilities. If made properly they can be as potent an adversary as any man. As smart as the person they were. As devious. As creative. As quirky. They have loyalty to Archdevils. They can work with the groups of fallen humans which are in the Archdevil's entourage. And they have enough left of their old personality to maintain the love of their friends and family. Because they maintain all this individuality, as you're seeing, they can occasionally backfire. But the Architect, or whomever or whatever designed them, did a damn fine job in making sure they're self-correcting.

"What happens is this. The joy you feel when you hear a baby laugh, or the warm feeling you get when you see a happy friend—they feel that too. The uplifting sensation of giving another person an unwarranted gift. The warmth of community. The power of love in a moment of consensual sex . . . they feel it all too—only backwards. They feel the calmness of a divine blessing when they hear a baby cry, or when their friend is wounded. They feel the uplift of charity when they steal. They feel the warmth of community when they collapse a civilization. They feel the eternal and unquenchable power of love in rape.

"And when they do give an unrequited gift, or help a person survive a calamity, they feel as guilty as you would, had you stolen or murdered.

"That's what the taint in their soul does to them. Now, so wights can work with the Archdevils and their cronies, so they can serve Minotaurs and Nephilim, some of the underpinnings of their morality have been left intact. Reciprocity, for instance, is still there. Giving a gift is repugnant, but a mutually beneficial trade can be done. If you do something for them, they feel as wretched as a normal person might for not having returned the favor . . . although for an opposite reason. Their empathy is something I'm not sure of. Maybe they have difficulty knowing what others feel because their frame of reference is so damaged. Maybe it's because the taint gets that too. I don't know, and nor did Kent, the infidel who wrote the most about them.

"Do you understand this so far?"

Did I?

I think over Q's words.

My son wants to murder kittens, and when he kills them, he'll feel like he rescued them.

"I got it," I say. "Go on."

"So your son is backfiring, which is good. This can

happen when you turn a nearly complete psychopath into a wight. They weren't rewarded or punished much for helping people anyway, so there is not a lot there to reverse."

I grunt. "So Aiden's a psychopath?"

Q sighs. "No, I don't think he's a psychopath. No one, as a rule, generally thinks of themselves as evil, but you do find people who commit atrocities thinking they're good. Inquisitors and missionaries and the like. Hell, Neb's a perfect example. Anyway, when you reverse those kinds of people, they can do great good, thinking it's evil. That dead stepfather of his, the Archdevil, convinced your boy of some very weird things. Your son thinks the way to torture a soul the most is to help it resist Hell. He thinks that if the soul gives up and lets itself die, it eventually comes to a place of peace. So in his mind, helping people resist Hell is causing them untold amounts of suffering, and *that* makes him feel good."

One of these days, Devil, I'm going to get my hands on you, and I'm going to make you pay for what you've done to me and mine.

"That's really fucked up," I say. "So if he hadn't turned wight, Xyn would have used him to kill people?"

"Right," Q says. "Aiden's stepfather was probably planning to let him go through puberty before turning him all the way."

"Why would he do that?"

Q rubs his hand over his head again. "Wights don't grow, Cris. He'd want a real weapon. An adult wight with all the size and strength that entails."

Fuck, I'm a father to a black-eyed Peter Pan.

Q sits up straight again. "Then, maybe when Aiden rebelled from teenage angst, he'd feed him the rest of the wight dust, and *viola*, a perfect wight."

Maybe. But Aiden had been on edge when I rescued him. Unless . . . unless a million things.

"So we just need to be careful not to argue with him about that," I say.

Q frowns. "Your son's smart. His mind is a little like yours, in a way. Good pattern recognition—but he's untrained. And like you, he resists that training out of stubbornness. But here's the thing I like about you most, Cris, and it's going to be a serious problem with him. You do change your mind. You learn the concepts that you disagree with, and then you apply them, and you change. It takes you a while, but you do it.

"Aiden is going to see a million little hints that he's wrong. Each time he helps a person resist Hell, that person is going to be happy. It's going to grate on him. Those hints will accumulate. Now if he were like Nebuchadnezzar, it wouldn't matter. Like you, Neb, and Cid, Aiden's capable of sustaining huge amounts of pain in order to do an overarching moral good—well, bad in his case, but you know what I mean. Unlike

Nebuchadnezzar though, and like you, I think Aiden is probably going to change his mind without something as powerful as the Infidel pushing him to do it."

I sit up and then cover my face with my hands.

The waterfall's rush isn't soothing enough for this shit.

"Will we have warning?" I ask.

I feel Q shift beside me. "I hope so. Aiden's very smart, but he is impulsive. He'll probably drop some hints."

"So we can keep him alive?"

A long moment passes before Q answers. "I told you in Maylay Beighlay, you need to let go. For a while I thought I was wrong, but it turns out this is something you're going to have to do. Let his time with you be a living mourning. When you can let him go, we should destroy him before he has a chance to hurt anyone."

"I can't let go, Q," I say.

"I know."

"How long?" I ask.

He stands up, pulling the devilwheat stalk out of his mouth and tossing it into the river. I watch the slow current carry it under the bridge.

"I don't know, Cris. I don't know."

"Anything else you can tell me?"

The weed, now on the far side of the bridge, dips for a moment below the water before resurfacing at a bend.

"This wight loves you. Aiden has the loyalty to you he must have held for his stepfather."

I try to process that, to use Q's knowledge to gain some understanding on the weirdly reversed tangle of fucked up rights and wrongs which must inhabit my son's head.

But in the end, does any of that matter?

He loves me.

And that's the ledge Hell has offered to stop my downward fall.

Which means I'll grab onto it. I'll cling to it for all it's worth.

Then it will crumble, and not even the strength of all the infidels will be able to stop me from sinking deeper and deeper and deeper.

Bile rises in the back of my throat with all my terrible anger.

XV

And I thought the first dinner we had with Neb was awkward.

My son stares at the plates of food as Q brings them out.

I can still hear Cid working in the kitchen.

"There are eating utensils in there," Q says to Aiden, pointing to the doorway. "I'd ask that you get some for each of us."

Aiden's black eyes regard him coolly. "I shouldn't be here."

Q shrugs. "Agreed. But so long as you *are* here, and eating, we'll ask for certain things in return."

Q said wights still felt the obligation of reciprocity.

He must be trying to use that to ensure my son's loyalty.

"I don't eat," Aiden says.

"Incorrect," Neb breaks in. "Wights do eat. And you're faster and stronger after you do."

Aiden sneers. "I don't eat what you eat."

Neb inclines his head. "That is true."

Q puts one of his slender-fingered hands onto Aiden's shoulder. "We have food you can eat. We are infidels. You know you must both fear us and trust us."

Aiden regards him for a moment. Then he gets up and walks toward the kitchen.

Q sits down at the table, as calm as ever.

Neb leans forward. "You ever tame a wight before?"

Q shakes his head. "Never, I just read about how in one of our books."

Neb looks at me. "Q's got a way with wights."

"He's my son, Neb. He's not some wight."

"I'm just saying your son's in good hands."

I hear Cid's soft humming from the room beyond along with the clinking of silverware. The song's not one I'd heard before. I keep expecting it to be familiar, for the notes to line up with something in my past, but they don't.

Aiden returns to the room, knives and forks in his hands. "I couldn't lift some of the knives. They wouldn't move."

Q nods. "You can't be stabbed by the knives you can't lift either, they are made of old world stuff. Your immunity gives you certain disadvantages, too."

I'm not sure how wise it is to give Aiden anything sharp, but Neb and Q seem perfectly at ease.

Well, I guess they should. If Aiden's going to kill, he'll start with me.

My son sets the utensils on the table, the forks to the left and the knives to the right. Now who taught him that? Here's to hoping it was his mother.

Cid enters with a set of plates. The food's aroma is causing my mouth to water, but my heart just isn't in this meal.

She places one plate in front of Aiden.

It's cooked . . . I don't know what it is, but it smells like . . . like a meat I know I've smelled before. I lean closer to it. Pork maybe? But how?

"This sauce is made with bits of harpy," Cid says as she puts a bowl by Aiden. "You've probably never had this kind of meat before, so you may want to try it without the sauce first."

Aiden's face is unreadable. He looks at her, unblinking.

"You are required to say thank you when we complete a transaction," Q says.

Aiden sneers. "Thank you."

Wait a minute.

I stand up and point to the pork-seeming stuff she

put in front of Aiden. "What is that, Cid?"

Cid sets her last plate down and takes a seat at the head of our table. "Sit down, Cris."

"No, you tell me what that is."

She sighs. "It's cooked fleshstone, Cris."

I fucking knew it. Fleshstone grows naturally in places. It's like rock, but it's made out of human flesh—and that's why I've smelled it before. I've seen dyitzu fire consume a man. Seen the flame melt his fat, send it bubbling up through his seared skin and had the smell of his death linger in my nostrils.

"That's not right, Cid!" I shout. "He's not eating that."

Cid looks up at me with her narrow green eyes. "We can't feed him normal food, Cris. He's a wight. It won't digest. If he's going to be healthy, if he's going to produce wight dust and have high levels of energy, this is necessary."

"It's fucking cannibalism, Cid."

She shakes her head. "First, if you have to eat a fallen comrade to survive, you do. Secondly, this isn't a fallen comrade. It's fleshstone. No one died."

I can't figure out infidels. They're moral asswipes in some places, but in others, it's like they don't care at all.

I put my fists on the table and lean forward. "I'm his fucking father, Cid. You rule the roost, but I choose what happens to him. I have a veto. You and I know that fleshstone is the same as human meat. It's wrong to eat it, Cid. There are fucking Greek myths about the horrid shit that happens when you cook humans and serve them to people."

"They're just myths, Cris," Neb says.

I turn on him. "You stay the hell out of this."

He holds up his hands and leans back in his chair.

Aiden is looking at the table. He hasn't taken his first bite yet.

Cid is grinning, and I can't understand why. I look around, seeing that we are caught in the grim mockery of some kind of old world dinner conversation.

"No," I say to Cid while pointing at the fleshstone. "This isn't funny, and it's *not* normal."

Cid starts laughing. After a moment, I realize that Q and Nebuchadnezzar are smiling too.

Cid holds up one hand. "We're eating a family dinner with a wight and a necromancer. It's extremely not normal. That ship," she straightens her arm emphatically, "has *sailed*."

Neb loses his composure next and gives out a belly laugh. Q is not far behind. I try to stay pissed, but staying angry is going to take more out of me than I have to give.

"You're right, he's your son," Cid says over the laughter. "If you want to veto, do it. I don't think we should even have a wight with us. But if we're going to do this, if we're going to have him as one of us, even if it's just for the trip back, then we should treat him as a teammate."

Aiden looks at me. I can tell he wants the meat.

If he eats it, he'll owe me. He has to owe me because if he doesn't, that means we have a bond of love. Love hurts him.

And he still gets hungry.

Oh, Devil, you fucked up. I'm going to use this. You wanted to have your cake and eat it too. You wanted an evil being that can form packs. Well I'm going to use that against you. I'm going to reclaim my son.

"Go ahead," I tell him.

And we eat.

Later that night, I find myself emotionally bewildered. I'm not sure if I'm euphoric or so depressed that I'm about to go still. After relieving myself, I stumble to the study.

Q and Cid are waiting for me there.

"Are you sure?" Cid is saying. "I don't know that he's in good enough shape for this. Keith's man might get more out of Cris than Cris gets from him."

Q looks at me. "You okay, cowboy?"

I don't know how to respond.

Q nods. "He's good."

Cid rolls her eyes. "I think it might be best if you just do another session, Q. Cris hasn't been taught shit about cooperative interviewing techniques. His idea of interrogation probably comes from syndicated TV shows."

I shrug. She's probably right.

Q puts one hand to his bald scalp. "It's worth a shot, Cid. This guy's afraid of Cris. I think Keith's whole crew is. He calls Cris 'the Godslayer' for some reason. Probably because he killed the Archdevil in Maylay Beighlay. There's something wrong with Keith's man. Seriously wrong. I've not questioned anyone quite so afraid."

Cid considers this, sighs, then gives me a wry look. "Alright, lover, you up for this?"

No. No, I'm probably not. "Sure."

Again my long shadow traverses a cell, falling this time upon the prisoner's face.

His thin frame is curled up into a close approximation of the fetal position—only medieval looking handcuffs bind his hands behind his back.

It's Fin.

He's unkempt, his brown hair and wispy beard disheveled. He's shaking, not so much a hyena now. Now he just seems like the cancer Cid once described the Order as.

"Godslayer," Fin says, and for some reason it seems to me like his voice is hopeful. "You've come for me!"

I'm not sure what to say, so I say nothing. The door slams behind me, and I'm left in nearly complete darkness. A triangle of light, creeping in under the door, makes its way a few inches into our chamber. I kneel in one corner, making the sign of the cross.

I don't know why I do it, but I figure it might scare Fin, so I do.

Then I sit down, my back to the corner, my legs pulled up. I rest my arms on my knees and bow my head.

"Keith tried!" the man screeches an apology. "He tried to resist it. We didn't know. You have to believe me! We didn't know."

I look up.

Q's right. Something is seriously fucked up with Fin, even compared to how unstable he was after Soulfall.

"We're not like that!" he goes on. "We don't deal with devils. You know we don't. You think raping is wrong . . . I know that. I *know* that. But you're wrong. You're fucking wrong, man. We don't deal with devils. Ever. We just didn't know."

"You dealt with Xyn," I observe.

"He was good! Cris. You fucking killed him, but he was good."

I feel cold air on the back of my neck.

"You dealt with *another* devil?" I ask.

He twists around, rolling onto his belly. "No!

Never with the devil. We don't. It was worse. Please! Please forgive me. Absolve me. Save me. Kill it. Kill it like you killed Xyn."

Forgive him for what, working with demons? Giving me to Igraine? Has this man gone completely insane or has his crew really struck a deal with another devil?

"Why is it that you think an infidel can offer you absolution?" I ask.

His eyes go wide. "Because you aren't one. Not really. We know that. Keith told us all about you. How you knew of Blood Pass."

I remember that conversation, after they'd captured me, when they tried to figure out who I was. Keith had put enough of the puzzle pieces together back then to figure out I couldn't have been an Infidel Friend.

"You know what I've killed," I say.

His head bobs frantically, his chin banging against the floor hard enough that I worry for his safety. "Yes! You killed Xyn, the Devil Reborn. You're more than an Angel. You're the Godslayer. I was angry at you, but you didn't do it to hurt us."

I stand. "I didn't."

His eyes are wide. "I knew it was true! I knew it! Xyn just got in your way. Please . . ."

I take a step toward him. "I will absolve you, but first you have to tell me what I want to know."

Fin rolls over to his back, laying on his bound

hands. "We followed you!" he shouts, spittle coming out of his mouth. "We chased you through the Pole and back to Dendra. We followed you through Portsmouth, and then—"

"I know, you followed me onto Soulfall."

"Yes!" he shouts. "We followed you. It was on Soulfall, waiting for us. We kept trying to go up, but we couldn't. Keith was in hysterics. He knew you'd made it to the second peak, but it didn't matter, there were no stairs up. We felt the darkness getting closer, but we had nowhere else to go! The dyitzu were behind us. We just went down, and down, and down."

His eyes are wide, frantic. He's in some kind of fucked up ecstasy, and I can see a boner forming in his pants. Drool spills out from the sides of his mouth, and I long for him to stop speaking because somehow, in some way, I know what he's going to say next.

"There was something down there!" he shouts his confession. "I could feel it. It's evil, Godslayer, pure evil. It's not from this Hell. It comes from the one beyond. And it was waiting for us." He begins crying. "We didn't know. I'm so sorry. The infidels are evil, they are, but they're not evil like devils. We'd help you fight it. We would have. We tried . . . too late."

My heart is beating madly in my chest. I want to step forward to comfort this man, or to kill this man, or to do something—anything, anything to stop him from talking.

Tears form in my eyes, and I can't explain why they're there. Some part of my mind has figured something out, but . . .

. . . but the words keep spewing out of his mouth. "There were things in Soulfall's halls, reflections of our minds, they were all fucked up. They tore into me. They planted seeds in our souls. Keith, he was the only strong one. He kept looking for a way out. There was this room, way far down, with clearsteel windows—you saw it. We could see back to the cliff. We beat on those windows, but they wouldn't give. That place . . . it was wrong. And we thought we lost Ryan. We did. But then he was there . . ." Fin stops. He's panting fast. He sits up quickly, spittle and tears flying. "*Then he was there.* And we were all . . . all heartened . . . but not Ryan. He seemed calm, distant. Ryan wasn't afraid of anything. We finally found a way up. We made progress. We found a way *out.*" He comes up to his knees. "Oh, Godslayer! We were free! We'd left the place behind. Durgan helped us capture you." His voice drops to a whisper, and he suddenly seems terribly sane. "We thought we had, we didn't know your power. But *it* was already with us when we found you, you see."

Then the answer hits me like a tsunami. "Ryan!" I blurt out.

His head bobs again, and this time it's the back of his skull which impacts with the hard stone floor.

Oh Keith, you poor stupid bastard.

"We didn't come back alone. We brought that something with us. It's not from here. It's from the next Hell. We could feel its evil. You were there. Surely you felt it. It drove Alec insane. When we looked back across the great divide, we saw the clearsteel windows. Ryan was still in there. Do you remember? Do you *understand?*"

Fin's on his feet now, a toothy grimace of fear plastered across his face, and he shouts at me. "Do you understand? You were with us! *Ryan was there, behind the glass, left behind.* He was beating on the glass, screaming as the dark things took his soul. But Ryan was also *next* to us. He had climbed out with us. *Do you understand?"*

My hands are shaking as I reach out to touch his shoulder.

His body trembles like a frightened animal.

"Do you understand?" He shouts. "We did something wrong. Something so wrong. I didn't mean it. Keith didn't. We just didn't know."

I guide him back to the floor, gently bringing him to his knees. "I understand. There was a darkness in Soulfall. We all felt it, too. You found it. You brought it back with you."

His wide eyes sparkle and his mouth is caught in some sort of rictus grin midway between pure joy and absolute terror. "After we traded you, Ryan kept changing. He got Igraine's trust. Ryan took us back to the river! Keith tried. He tried to fight it, to keep us sane. But it tortured us. It kept us by the Erebus and laid seeds in us. Keith said you would kill it. He told it that. He told it you were coming for it, the Godslayer. The Angel of God sent from Heaven to protect Myla. The man who slew the Devil Reborn. But . . . you don't understand it. It took Ryan's body. At first it was like Ryan. But as the days passed, Ryan changed. You were there. Ryan rotted away and it was waiting underneath."

He goes on, about torture on Soulfall, about Keith, about this and that. About how Ryan commanded the evil spirits of the Erebus. I have no idea what parts of his story come from his diseased mind or what parts might be real, but I'm pretty sure of one thing.

When Keith's team left Soulfall, they did not come back alone.

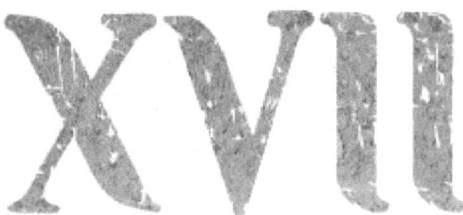

Q paces back and forth after I give them the best account I can of Fin's insane ramblings. Neb sits, his blond head in his hands, his blue eyes staring at his boots.

El Cid chews her lip.

No one is happy with the news.

Q stops. "We don't know how long they were on Soulfall. Keith and his men could be laboring under a delusion. They might have been driven insane there, and this man only thinks they brought something back."

"They were fucked up when they had me, Q," I say, "but not *this* fucked up."

Neb lifts his head. "There was something down there, Q. I felt it."

Q frowns. "Soulfall was dark, Neb. It's easy to feel things that—"

"I felt it too," Cid says. "We all felt the same thing. Our feelings on Soulfall are not like our feelings in the old world, where a bit of low blood sugar might fool some new age twat into believing in ghosts. It's not just a vague sense of malaise set upon us from our environs. We all felt the evil from the same direction. On Soulfall, feelings aren't always simply a reaction to our senses, they themselves can be a sense. If our senses give us the same input, and we have verification, then it's something we need to take seriously."

Q paces again and after two laps, stops. "But we don't have verification."

The Nazi leans back and crosses his black-booted legs. "Maybe we do."

Q's eyebrows raise. "You mean the insane man's testimony?"

Cid shakes her head. "There's a detail that bugs me. He could have hallucinated it, he could have made it up, but it accurately describes a process most people don't know can happen."

Neb's blue eyes are locked on Cid. "You mean the body changing. You think it might be a Revenant."

"Yes," Cid says. "The Infidel told you about that?"

"I struck a pretty good bargain," Neb says. "He

gave me a *lot* of information in exchange for my continued separation from Nephysis and Lucreas."

Q nods, but I sure as hell don't know what they're talking about.

"What do you mean by the body changing?" I ask. "I can verify that it's true. Ryan was both next to us and behind the glass. Is there some kind of shape shifter devil?"

Cid shakes her head. "If only it were that simple. No. There's a way to get souls from Sheol back into Gehenna. It's not easy, and we infidels have never been able to pull it off. The Archdevils, though, they have ways of reaching across the levels of Hell and communicating. When a person has the stilling in Gehenna, their soul is wandering around in Sheol. The body is empty, but it has this leftover connection to its soul. Very rarely, a soul comes back into the body. . . but it doesn't always have to be the soul that left it. Another soul, if it catches onto that connection, can come back."

"You're fucking kidding me," I say.

Q leans back against a wall. "She's not. A body can hold a soul. The weird part is that the soul still has to flow through a person's brain. So for a while, that person will seem the same . . . but Hell heals all wounds, Cris, including brain damage. Slowly, the host's body will heal into the parasite's body. The host's brain will heal into the parasite's brain"

Neb grunts. "So you do need to take this seriously."

But something doesn't fit. "I saw their guy, back on Soulfall, beating against a window. Maybe the bodies swapped places? Or that was Ryan's soul trying to escape?"

Cid frowns. "No, neither of those possibilities make sense. None of our explanations account for that detail."

"So we might be safe," Neb says. "It's entirely possible the Soufall Ryan was a projection or a shade, and we're just being tracked by a bunch of madmen—*not* a soul from Sheol."

Cid crosses her arms. "Agreed. That's also a possibility we need to take seriously."

Cid is abnormally forward tonight—which believe me, is saying something. I don't know what's gotten into her. She strips with infidel quickness.

Her hands are all over me, tugging at my clothes.

I stop her.

Her eyes are sad, like a puppy dog's. She pants, her small breasts rising and falling, their erect nipples practically quivering in the dim light.

"No foreplay?" I ask her.

She grins like a school girl and shakes her head quickly.

She dives in again, her hard lips pressing into mine. She unbuttons my pants and shoves them down. I barely have time to get erect before she lowers herself onto me.

She fucks me enthusiastically for what seems like hours. When she's had her fill, she gets off and sits on the stone, a contented smile on her face.

"What got into you?" I ask.

She giggles. "I'm proud of you, Cris. I can kind of see what you might become someday, and it makes me giddy to think about it."

I think of the latest series of my outright failures. "I think you're nuts. I've been pretty shitty lately. Something may have escaped from Soulfall. A single wrong word to Aiden can set him against us."

Her quizzical eyes regard me. "Hell takes all things from us eventually."

"And that doesn't depress the fuck out of you?"

"On some nights it does," she admits. "On others, when I can lie in the safety of a lover's arms, I feel a different way."

"I try to just let go, Cid. I try. I really try. I know I need to, but I can't."

Now her eyes are sorrowful. "I know."

"They fucked me, Cid. In Igraine's palace. They fucked my brain up more than my body."

"I know."

"Save me, Cid. Make it right. Make all of this right."

"I will, lover. I don't know how, but I will."

XVIII

Before coming to the complex, I'd not tried to read a book in over a decade. I don't remember reading being this tiring. It's like my eyes don't want to focus on the tiny infidel letters. And it doesn't help that the letters themselves are shaped funny. Nor does it help that the damn book they asked me to read was written in 18th century English.

Neb is having a better time of it.

My head hurts like hell.

I consider reading in the garden, but I'm afraid of that place.

I close my eyes, and the dull ache behind them seems better.

With a snort, I slam the book shut, not even remembering what page I was on.

I put the book on one of the shelves and move to the staircase.

Neb, diligently reading, looks up. "Where are you going?"

I shake my head helplessly. "It's been too long. My head hurts. I'm headed someplace . . . someplace dark."

I crawl down the ladder into the watch room, closing the hatch behind me.

It's possible I was a little distracted and that's what made focusing difficult. Even with a clear mind, I'm sure I would've had a headache. I mean, reading is like a muscle right? I hadn't exercised that particular muscle since the old world.

I sit back against a corner and close my eyes.

But sure, if I'm honest with myself, the distractions are getting to me. Not any guilt, of course. Just stress. Aiden is, well, he is what he is. I'm not sure how much of that I can salvage. And there's some insane people out there, enemies driven mad by Soulfall—or by something darker. It makes sense that I'm feeling pressure. There's nothing to be ashamed of. Maybe I should feel guilty for misjudging Cid. Maybe I should feel guilty because I'm not willing to kill my son.

Worse than that, I'm pushing the infidels to make the wrong decision too. And they're willing to do it.

They love me so much they're willing to do it.

The stone beneath me is cool.

I open my eyes.

Staring through that crystal no longer scares me. Aiden's not out there. He's not alone. Whatever torture he'll feel, he's not alone. And Q said it. He said it so long ago. Sometimes when a person is in a lot of pain, you have to put them down. If the suffering is too much, or if that suffering will hurt others, sometimes that's the only solution. Not often, but sometimes it is.

I'm sorry, Aiden. I held on too long, and you're the one who paid for it.

I'm just lucky I haven't gotten my friends killed. Had they been anything but infidels, I'm sure we'd all be dead. Me, Neb, and Aiden. We're a match for parts of Hell, sure, but could normal people have traveled that river and fought their way through Soulfall?

That's what I'll do. I'll go and tell Cid I'm ready to make the right decision.

It's time to kill Aiden.

Only I can't move.

I've cried so much over the last few weeks, more than I have in my entire life. More than I did even when Myla had stolen my son. And here I am, crying again.

I've got to pull myself together.

Somewhere, somehow, I'd lost faith in myself.

No, that's not quite right. I've started caring about who I am. Before I didn't give a damn.

Let them all die. Let Hell fall to pieces. But my son . . . no. What am I thinking?

I was never like that. That was Myla. She was the one willing to damn the millions to help our son. I couldn't do it. Even without infidel training or logic, my heart wouldn't let me betray humanity.

I wonder what must have gone so horribly wrong in hers. .

And was any of that my fault?

It had to be.

Look at how I betrayed Cid's trust. Surely I did worse to Myla.

So what the hell am I going to do to pay Cid back? How do I become the kind of person who *can* pay her back? Who won't betray her?

While I ponder this, I let my eyes run across the stone in the chamber beyond the crystal. Maybe I can see one of those things Q showed me, one of the veins within veins. There's not a lot of skystone in there, so I'm not likely to see much. Still, I can make out the grain of the hellstone. I try to find a pattern in it, letting my mind open up and intuitively feel out its nature.

Maybe there is a flow.

Maybe not.

Maybe the hellstone is too . . . quiet? Maybe I'd have to excavate the cavern to find its secrets.

Or maybe if I could see past the person in my way out there, I could tell. His dark grey clothes almost meld in with the stone. He's hairless, too—hell, he doesn't even have eyebrows.

I start, then jump to my feet.

That man's eyes, they're on me—as if he can see me through the crystal.

Oh Jesus Christ.

It's a coincidence, it has to be. There's no way he can see me.

Another man walks across the room. And another. And another.

The hairless one's eyes are still locked on mine. But . . . he *can't* see through the crystal. I know he can't.

And there's Keith, a white shock in his otherwise black hair. Sure as shit, that's Cid's sword at his belt.

Oh no.

Oh fucking no.

God damn it.

I watch Keith and several men slink across the room—so many men, most of them Carrion born—and they keep coming. I recognize Harris amongst them, and there's Din, a dog at his heel.

Jesus. How many soldiers does Keith have? Do they know how to find us in our sanctuary?

But you know what? Let them come. I'm getting sick of this Hamlet-style-sitting-around-and-thinking-about-my-feelings bullshit, anyway.

I charge over to the ladder. With quick steps I climb and then push open the hatch.

I call as loud as I dare, "Q!"

"I see them through the periscope!" he shouts. "Cid, we've got company."

"It's Keith!" I call, abandoning caution. Q probably hasn't seen him yet.

"You're kidding me!" Cid's voice is more distant. "How many?"

Q doesn't answer.

"Not sure," I say.

I go down a couple of rungs to check.

God, they're still coming. And then I see him again, the hairless one, crouching in the corner. His eyes are directly on me. He's not staring at the crystal wall, he's not staring at where I was sitting a moment ago. He's staring directly at me.

I stick my head back through the hatchway. "One of them can see me!"

I duck down again to get a better look.

"That's impossible," Cid yells back.

I look through the wall, but he's gone. He must have followed some of his soldiers out of the room.

The parade of them is getting thicker.

"At least fifty, and they're not letting up!" I shout.

"He can see me too," Q's voice has a catch in it.

"What?" Cid is shouting back.

"The man Cris reported, he can see me too."

"He can't see you through the scope!" Cid says.

I climb out of the watch room and close the hatch

behind me.

"I'm telling you, Cid," Q insists. "I don't know how it's possible. I'm just telling you that it's happening."

I spin the lock.

"An infused," Cid shouts back.

I don't know what that is. I don't fucking know what's going on.

"Not possible." It's Q's turn to be in denial.

"Move!" Cid yells. "Get Neb and Cris to the armory, get them armored and armed. Fast. I'm going to have to drop it."

Drop it? The armory? Like out of the complex?

I run up the spiral stairs.

A blast shakes the complex and I stumble. I catch myself with my hands, the sharp edge of a step digging into my outstretched palms. My legs pump, propelling me forward. My hurt hands scramble briefly over the steps as I regain my footing.

I hear boots coming down from a level or so above. They better be fucking Neb's.

"It's Cris!" I shout as I come up.

Q's standing at the armory's doorway above a pile of weapons and clothes, my pack in his hand. "Suit up, load up!" he says. "No time."

"Neb and Aiden, coming down!" I hear Neb's German-accented voice announce.

The former Nazi bursts into the room, Aiden in tow.

The Icanitzu-hide clothes seem like they'll be tight, so I strip. No time for shame now.

Nebuchadnezzar shrugs off his overcoat and does the same.

I tug on the pants and shirt, hoping like Hell I didn't grab any of Neb's armor. I tuck a few boxes of shotgun shells into my pack.

Another blast shakes the complex and dust falls from the ceiling.

"How could he see us?" I shout.

Q, his M-16 at his shoulder, shakes his head. "I don't know, Cris."

I jam a host of M-16 clips into my pack.

Neb is putting his overcoat back on over his clothes. He picks up some clips too, sliding them into his pockets.

Q had stacked up some 9mm clips as well. I love that man.

I shove them in.

And infidel fire.

I *really* love that man.

I drop those into a side pocket.

Another blast.

I zip up the pack and shoulder it. Q's grabbed a pair of gladii, each one sheathed on a belt. He tosses one to Aiden. My son is able to catch it, so the swords must be hellforged. That's good because if Durgan is out there, I'll want something hellforged to stab him with.

Q slides the second sword down between my back and my pack, then fastens the sword's belt across my chest.

"Clear the armory!" Cid yells.

Q passes me an M-16, closes the door and steps back. "We're all clear."

I hear the sound of stone grinding. Another blast.

Gunfire echoes in from above.

"They've breached!" Q shouts.

More gunfire, the three-shot bursts of Cid's M-16.

"Go down!" I hear Cid shouting from above.

"Down down down!"

We rush to the stairs.

"But the exit's at the top!" Neb shouts, stopping in the stairwell's entrance.

"Down!" Q yells.

"There's too many!" Neb insists. "We need to run!"

Q shoves him through the doorway. "Ask not, soldier! Do!"

Neb runs down. Q and Aiden follow. I take the rear, angling myself sideways, looking up, my M-16 raised and ready.

I hear more gunfire and another blast.

"Cid!" Cid announces herself.

She comes around a curve, catching up with us. "Go go go!"

She's got the rear now, so I turn and dash down the stairs.

We stop at the entrance of the basement.

"Now what?" Neb yells.

"Hold the stairwell," Cid orders.

I flip my safety off. Everyone I don't want to kill is behind me.

Q and I kneel at the base of the steps and aim upward.

I see some feet coming down, so I shoot them. Blood spurts from where my three-round burst hit. A grey-shirted Carrion born comes falling forward. Q puts a bullet in his head.

The Carrion born was armed with a shotgun, which is probably a great weapon for fighting in these conditions.

I hear the spinning of the watch room's lock.

"Is there a way out of there?" I ask Q.

Showers of bullets and buckshot come down the stairwell. They must be hoping to hit us with ricochet, but they aren't that lucky. And hell, even if they get that lucky, I have this infidel armor on.

"Is there a way out?" I shout.

I hear the whistles of infidel fire canisters behind me.

What's Cid doing?

"Not yet," Q yells, ducking forward.

The whistles fade away, I'm assuming because Cid is dropping them into the watch room. I hear the padded thump of the door closing and the spin of the lock.

Another foot edges down the stairs. This time there's a hand with a pistol beside it. He must be bent over.

Q shoots the hand and I shoot the foot. I put the final bullet in the Carrion born's head as he tumbles. He lands on his dead friend.

The floor shakes with Cid's explosions and one of the bodies rolls down another step.

"Egress!" Cid shouts.

We stand back up.

Smoke is coming up through the now open hatch. Neb and Aiden drop into that smoke.

Q follows, diving through.

As I mount the ladder I hear another whistle, but this one ain't ours.

Cid jumps on me, her weight pushing me down. The smoke of her previous explosions stings my eyes. I hear the thud of the hatch closing and then there's another blast.

They've got infidel fire too?

Fuck these guys.

I try to slide down the ladder but slip, landing in a heap with Cid on top of me. Thank god she's light. I can't see shit. Smoke is everywhere. I struggle to my feet. I hear crystals grinding into the hellstone beneath my boots. I feel Cid's hand in mine.

She leads me through the smoke, through the

shattered crystal and ironglass wall, out into Hell.

XIX

The green skystone overhead covers us with its eerie light as Cid takes us forward into the wilds, smoke from the explosion still misting off her shoulders.

I see another grey clad man.

Fuck, they're out here too?

I fire a three-shot burst, and the right side of his shoulder releases a spurt of blood. I'd missed his center. Cid's aim is sharper, and the man drops.

"Form up, room clearing!" Cid orders. "Me and Cris up front. Q and Neb in back. Aiden, stay between us."

We haven't trained much, but for some reason I know I can handle this. Our steps become measured as we slow our pace. My torso becomes a stable platform for my weapon.

We breach the next few rooms.

I see a man as I burst through. True to my training, I ignore him, and scope the rest of the chamber. Cid fells him.

Nothing in my sights.

"Clear!" I say.

"Clear," Cid calls.

"All clear," Q replies.

I feel Aiden's small form behind me.

Cid and I push forward.

"How many can there be?" I ask.

"Keith's been busy," Cid says.

I notice the subvein in the ceiling which Q had showed me earlier.

"Cid," I warn. "This is where we left the false trail."

She nods. "I know. They clearly found it and figured it's false. Maybe they didn't leave people to ambush us this way."

The skystone turns more yellow, so I know we're getting close to the bridge room. Here, just ahead. I think that's it.

But for all Cid's fancy thinking, we still encounter the enemy, five of them.

Training be damned, we're outnumbered.

I charge into the room, loosing bullets, but missing my target narrowly. Cid gets out two bursts right after me. I hear Q's gun going off, but I'm not sure who he's shooting at. Cid dives to the floor. It's not cover, but it makes her a smaller target. I drop a pair with my next try, catching the second one in the head. One of the darkly dressed men levels a shotgun at me.

Cid hits him, and his gun blast goes off as he pitches forward.

Stones and buckshot fill the air by my head. Gravel and dust explode from the wall.

We got them!

But Q is still firing back down the tunnel behind us.

Neb is too.

"Up the bridge!" Cid yells. "Aiden, go!"

I follow my son across the room, hopping over a dead body.

"One at a time!" Cid yells.

But the hell with that. I pick up my son and charge up the bridge.

I hear a high whistle.

"They're suicidal," Q yells.

I flatten myself against the high landing which leads out of the room, covering Aiden with my body. The explosion goes off.

Shotguns and pistols boom, but they are soon met with the quick reports of our M-16s.

I hear more whistles. Darkly dressed men carry canisters in their hands, charging at us. The hell is wrong with them? Why don't they just throw their explosives? Cid and Q are shooting them down.

Fiery explosions rock the tunnel and shrapnel scatters across the chamber.

"Drop the bridge, Cris!" Q yells. "We'll meet you in the crystal room!"

He, Cid, and Neb make for another exit, firing furiously at the kamikaze Carrion born. All of these people can't have gone to Soulfall, so what's screwed up their heads? I creep forward, staying low, trying to keep out of sight.

From the sound of the gunfire, it seems like some of the Carrion born are shooting at my friends from under the bridge. I reach into the side pouch on my pack and remove a canister of infidel fire. I unscrew the top and drop it over the edge.

I hear it whistle. The men beneath me scatter, and they're cut down by Q, Neb, and Cid's bullets. The explosion goes off.

Smoke and dust fill the room, and I hear a tremendous crack.

I'm pretty sure the bridge collapsed.

Then another crack, and then a boom.

Well, it's definitely down now.

I spring to my feet, and Aiden's right there with me, his black eyes flashing. If he's feeling any emotion, his face isn't betraying it.

Together, we rush through the room's upper exit.

A shotgun booms as we cross one chamber.

There's three of them.

I leap for cover behind a jut of rock rising from the floor. I fire, but my M-16 is dry. Fuck, my clips are in the pack, and I sure as hell don't have time to unzip the thing and go searching for one.

I hear the footsteps of the men advancing.

Where's my son?

I draw the .22 from the small of my back and jump up, firing.

They're advancing carelessly across the room. Like Q said, suicidal.

I drop two, but again, my aim is off, and I hit the

last guy in the arm as I empty the gun. Oh shit, that's Clement. I hate that bastard. His shotgun booms, once, twice as he moves laterally across the chamber. I have to scurry around my cover to stay out of his line of fire.

I hear a scuffle and then Aiden gives a quick shout.

My heart freezes for a moment in my chest.

Fuck.

Silence.

Have I been hit? I see some blood dripping down my armor. I don't feel anything. Maybe it's someone else's blood.

"I've got your damn boy, Godslayer," Clement says. "Come on out. I don't need to kill you so bad. I just gotta take you to our master."

Melvin's stubble-filled face comes to my mind, and I remember Fellman's arms wrapped around my body. I will not be taken alive.

My hands are shaking.

But he's got my son. I'll do anything for Aiden, even face that again.

With a deep breath I steel myself. Their willingness to commit suicide gives them no advantage over me. I am as ready to die as they.

I dare a peek over my cover. Clement is hunched down, strands of his long blond hair falling in front of his eyes. He's got one arm around Aiden's throat and with his other hand he's pressing a pistol into my son's head.

Oh you dumb bastard. You poor, poor dumb bastard.

"I ain't got shit to tell Keith!" I shout back.

He issues a low, menacing chuckle. "Keith's not our leader anymore."

Oh. Right.

It's that damn thing that could see me through the crystal. The one Cid said was infused. The one that might be from Sheol—or as I'd known him, Ryan.

The chamber of my empty .22 gapes open, and my extra clips are all zipped up in my pack. Could I open one pocket and grab more ammo without alerting Clement?

I hear scuffling footsteps as the man drags my son toward me. I take another quick look and readjust, keeping this boulder between us.

"Come out," Clement says, "or I'll kill your boy. You don't understand what's going on. You can't imagine what's happened to us."

"Kill him, I don't fucking care," I shout back at him.

He gives that low chuckle again. "I know more about you, now, Godslayer. You may have been sent to Hell by God, but God's got no power here. I know you're bluffing. You won't let your boy die. You traveled from the Pole to Soulfall to save him."

A grin spreads across my face.

They really don't know. They really don't know my

son's a wight.

"I failed, Clement." I stand up from behind the boulder, my pack in my hands. "My son is dead."

He stops, and then peers down at Aiden, as if seeing him for the first time.

Clement shrieks.

I pull out the Old Lady.

Clement's face is blanched, his mouth agape as he regards the black orbs that are my son's eyes. He fires his pistol, but the bullet stops impotently at my son's temple, then falls, bouncing off of his shoulder before tinkling across the floor. Clement's familiar with Durgan, so he should have known better, and that sudden instinctual reaction costs him his life.

I let off a blast at his head.

His body tumbles to the ground. I bend down and retrieve my M-16, slinging it over one shoulder.

I hold out my hand.

Aiden steps over the dead man at his feet and takes it.

Hand in hand, we leave.

There are three more in the crystal room, and they must have heard the shooting earlier because they're ready for us. I drop back out of the chamber as soon as I see them. Their bullets race past me, impacting against the far wall.

Aiden draws his gladius and stands in the

entranceway. "Me first."

Their bullets fly, but they do little more than put tears in his clothes. The rounds drop to his feet, bouncing off the ground. One rolls, spent, stopping at my boot.

Aiden walks in with an unhurried pace.

I hear their shouts of alarm. "A wight!"

I follow in after, my shotgun booming. Aiden has cut one down, having slashed the man's throat. My first target drops. The only remaining Carrion born has a pistol. Had he any sense, he would have dived for cover. I blast him in his gun arm. He spins and falls, his piece skittering across the stone floor.

I rush up to him and put the Old Lady in his face.

"What's wrong with you bastards?" I shout. "Why are you trying to die?"

He's in pain, a lot of it. With a shout, he turns and reaches toward his all-too-distant pistol.

I drop one knee onto his buckshot riddled arm, pinning it, while I let my other knee land on his belly. The Old Lady's barrel slams into his face, knocking him back.

He shouts in pain.

"Tell me!" I order.

He curls up under my weight.

I jam the Old Lady into his eye. "Tell me!"

"It came from the rock," he says.

"What?"

He's bleeding arterially. He doesn't have much time.

I nudge him with the barrel of the Old Lady again. "What came from the rock?"

"Callodax," he says, his voice strained. "He'll take Londinium. He's Mithras."

I ease up a little, taking some of my weight off his torso.

I have no idea what he's saying, but maybe this shit will make sense to my buddies. "Go on."

"Igraine, she gave us to him . . . but . . . the dust. Keith tried to warn us. He tried to warn Igraine, but we didn't understand what he meant. Ryan, he changed. Keith tried . . ."

I feel the hairs on the back of my neck rise. "Igraine didn't listen?"

He shakes his head. "Keith told us what happened at Soulfall. He meant for us to know . . ."

Aiden jerks at my side. I look to him. He's afraid.

Fuck.

I remember so clearly the malice which rose up from the depths of that fallen city.

"His hair was coming out. Sometimes he was Callodax. Sometimes he was Ryan. Igraine, she made a deal with him . . ."

That's what Cid wanted, consistency and confirmation.

Wordlessly, I blow the man's face off. I walk back

to the crystal wall and rest against it. The undead claw at me from the far side. Cid should be here soon.

She'll know what to do.

She'll know what the thing Ryan has become, what Callodax is.

She'll know how to kill it.

Aiden walks up to the crystal wall, his gladius in one hand, his other outstretched. The undead don't care about him, of course.

He's one of them.

"Reload your weapons," Aiden says, "more Carrion men may be coming."

Blood drips off the point of his gladius.

His black eyes regard the wall.

Well, Keith, you're not the only one with a monster. I do as my son suggested. After emptying the M-16 earlier, though, I figure I need a better system. I put my 5.56 clips in a side pocket where they're easier to reach.

"Father," Aiden says, "he's here."

The thrill I feel at him calling me father is quickly replaced by terror.

Aiden's black eyes stare through the crystal.

I see it through the transparent wall, the infused man, the abomination, the malevolence from another Hell—Callodax. He's hairless, eyebrowless, weaponless, and clad all in the same dark grey Ryan had worn. While I can't see what color his eyes are in the dim light,

I can tell that they are not the black orbs of a wight or a dyitzu, nor the red of an Archdevil. They are human eyes, all too human eyes, but the undead do not touch him.

He stands in their midst, an island of stillness in the desperate clawing sea of undead.

Callodax's physiognomy is sharp, and the bald head gives his features a look of supreme malevolence. So far removed from Soulfall, I can't quite sense the malice he must carry, but I can certainly remember it.

I rise to face him.

Not more than a foot of crystal wall separates us. His eyes are on my son.

I tap the crystal twice with my Old Lady. The undead go crazy, scratching mercilessly against the clear rock. One's fingers, weakened from death, break, bending sideways.

The infused's eyes focus on me.

My breath leaves a tiny amount of condensation on the crystal, and it fades away. Comes back, and fades away. Comes back, and fades away.

"You can hear me, can't you?" I ask the evil thing.

He doesn't respond in any way, but I bet he can. He could see me before, so I figure his senses are ridiculously sharp. Callodax's eyes return to my son. Aiden edges closer to me, and in a strangely human gesture, clings to my arm.

"No, you look at *me!*" I say, and I tap the Old Lady

into the crystal again.

He does.

I sheath the Old Lady. "I don't know what you are," I tell it. "I don't know where you're from. But I know what I am, and I know where I'm from. I am the Godslayer. I was sent here on a holy mission to rescue my former lover. I am an infidel, and if you come after my son, you will die. I will pick your ass up and drag you back to the Erebus and hold you there until a Fury disembowels you. Do you understand me?"

No response.

The condensation on my side of the crystal comes and goes and comes and goes.

There's none on his side. I'm not sure if he's not breathing, or if he's just farther away from the wall than me.

"Cid," I hear El Cid announce herself.

"Q."

"Neb."

El Cid comes to a halt when she sees the infused. "Oh, shit."

Does she recognize him?

"Cris," she says, her voice wavering as she speaks my name, "we have to go."

So we run.

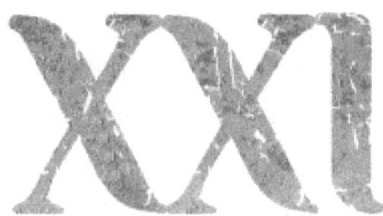

"Swords only," Cid says, jogging by me.

I follow. "Why?"

"Swords don't run out of bullets," she answers.

She takes us at an even pace, just below a run, through the tunnels. Her infidel sense of direction is uncanny. We never double back. We never meet a dead end. We never seem lost.

And we never stop.

The miles disappear behind us.

Just as before, when we rowed at top speed down the Northern Lethe, the devils are surprised to see us.

Cid leads the way, gladius flashing.

Q follows in her wake, his purple sword whipping

back and forth.

Neb, Aiden and I come after. Usually there's not much left for us to handle.

Thank God I had time for my ankle to get better.

I don't think I've ever run this far in my life.

My undead son is unflagging. No sweat issues from his body. No fatigue shows on his features. The infidels are just as stoic, but a little more sweaty. We journeymen, me and Neb, are the ones struggling.

At times Q drops back to scout. He returns quickly using energy reserves which seem inhuman to me.

Neb and I start to trail farther and farther behind.

"I'm . . . I'm," Neb pants, "I need a . . . break."

My shoulders have been rubbed raw by the bouncing of my pack, the sheath of the gladius is steadily burrowing into my back, but, thanks to Jessica's well-made footwear, my feet are fine.

"I'll tell her," I say.

Drawing on my will more than my muscles, I increase my pace.

The caverns are still semi-natural, but the walls are starting to show more evidence of brickwork. I think this means we're trending away from the Northern Lethe.

The next room has a floor made of skulls. They crunch under my feet, sending puffs of bone dust into the air. I catch up with Cid halfway through the room.

"How long . . . until we rest?" I ask between

breaths.

Her black hair, tied into a pony tail, bounces back and forth, landing on her pack and rising again with each stride. "We won't rest soon."

"Neb's tired," I say.

We enter another room with a floor full of skulls. Our feet crush them again. It occurs to me that we're not doing much to hide our trail.

"He can fall behind if he wants," she says. "I wouldn't recommend it."

No shit.

"Are they still . . . behind us?" I ask.

"Yes," Q answers.

Our next room has cobblestones instead of skulls. That's an improvement at least.

"Do you . . . know . . . what we . . . are fighting?" I ask.

"Get Neb a wrap," Cid tells Q.

Q drops back.

Oh damn, the wraps. I'd loved them when I'd eaten them, but for some reason, the idea of swallowing another one makes me feel sick.

"What's the plan . . . Cid?" I ask.

"We run."

"What's an . . . infused." It almost costs me too much breath to speak.

"They . . . a Minotaur can strengthen a person's body. An Archdevil can do the same thing . . . except in a person's soul . . . so it doesn't wear off. That's how infused are made. Infused can . . . I don't know. We run."

The next room has a forest of ten yard wide pillars shooting up into an abyss of blackness that hovers hundreds of feet above our heads. I can't tell if they connect to the ceiling or not.

Cid leads us through them, weaving two and fro, her pace undiminished. "We need to get on a river to lose him. If we have too, we'll take one that leads down into the Carrion. Our best bet is to come up through Dendra . . . and get to the Kingsriver. It's got enough forks that we can lose him, and we'll have to have a good lead so that he can't pick up our scent in the air."

Jesus. "He can . . . smell us?"

Cid shrugs as she runs. "That's my guess. He's behind us still, somehow. And his men, they're messed up. I think this one . . . he's different."

"I questioned . . . one of the Cancer," I tell her between frantic gasps for air. "He said Ryan . . . was changing. Said he was . . . Callodax one second, Ryan the next. Callodax is . . . the infused guy's name."

She looks at me, her green eyes flashing. "Do you think he was telling the truth?"

I nod.

"The next time Neb gets tired," she says, "tell him that. Tell him the thing chasing us isn't just an infused, it's a thing from Sheol. A Revenant. He won't need a wrap."

Cid increases our pace.

We rest in brief spurts, but we're always interrupted by Q or Cid, who come running in with news of our approaching enemies. Time is impossible to measure, and I'm not sure if I'd count the anxiety ridden state my body falls into as sleep.

I see Cid and Q exchanging looks sometimes, when one returns. Because they alternate as our warning, they rest only half as much as Neb and I, and yet, their tiredness is of a lesser sort. What's in those shared glances? At what point do we accidentally trigger that infidel response which demands they abandon us.

But looking at my indefatigable son who trots beside us, who by all my understandings of infidel behavior should not be alive, I wonder if that time will ever come. No, probably not. My Nazi friend and I are the anchors, and if we can't run fast enough, we will drag our infidels down into death.

The changes in Hell are subtle. At first, there seems to be a light haze in the air. Then we come to chambers which I could call misty. Here a great root has breached the floor before spiraling up into the ceiling. And now the fog is so thick I can't see the back wall.

A lichen-like substance coats some rocks, and moss covers others.

My nipples have been rubbed raw, and I'm almost positive they're bleeding under my infidel armor. My pack's bouncing has pulped my shoulders. I had not thought it possible for people to run for so long. When I try to figure out how much ground we've covered, it boggles my mind. Surely this is farther than I've ever run before.

Is it Hell that gave me this sudden stamina? Fear?

I am breathing as hard as I can, as quickly as I can. Black spots form in my vision.

It won't be long before I simply fall unconscious.

Both Neb and I have long since sheathed our gladii. Not a very infidel thing to do, but we don't really have the energy to fight anyway.

Cid comes to a halt.

This scares me because she hasn't said anything about a rest period. If I quit running now, I know there's no way I'll be able to get myself going again. But she's our leader, so I stop.

She walks into the next room. Q and Aiden follow her, but I stay back, panting. They pause at a wall of light shining in the mist.

Neb catches up with me. Except for Aiden, we're all out of breath and covered in sweat, but Neb looks the worst. He collapses.

I try to beg for help, but I can't find my voice between my breaths, so I limp into the shining room after Cid.

There is no way to tell how large this chamber is. All I'm sure of is that we have come out of the side of a cliff. The wall behind us is all we can see both above and below. Ahead, there is only mist. Up, only mist. Down below the ledge—you get the idea.

"Rest," Cid says, "then we climb. These chambers should look familiar. At the end of our ascent, we should make it to Dendra."

I collapse. Vaguely, I feel someone, either Q or Cid, shaking my legs, I guess to make sure I don't cramp up—that's awful nice of them. Awful nice.

El Cid rises silently through the thick fog which obscures her features from my vision. "There will be devils in the mist." Her voice is soft.

I feel the soreness in my muscles as I fight to stand. After a moment, I succeed.

Q rouses Neb and drags the exhausted necromancer to his feet.

Aiden, eyes open, stands up from his crouch.

Cid has no weapon at the ready. Her M-16 is strapped to her back. Her right hand though, hangs next to her pistol.

"We're about to go for a long climb," Q says quietly. "This isn't going to be like Eden chamber. We don't have time to use carabiners. Check the knots in your bootlaces. Keep your sidearm handy, but keep your hands free. Balance first, fire second. With your packs, check to make sure your things are stowed carefully and will not shift—then make sure they are on tight, as tight as you can get the straps. And don't skimp on the waist strap, that's the most important part. Follow Cid's lead. Stay close because the mists are thick. It will be easy to get lost. And don't fall."

After getting Jessica's shoes tied up and my gear ready, I sling my pack onto my bruised shoulders. With clumsy fingers I tighten the straps around my shoulders and waist, tugging on the straps until they hurt.

I follow Cid as she steps onto a ridge which runs along the side of the cliff wall. It's narrow, *really* narrow, perhaps only six inches wide in some places. Behind me comes Neb, then Aiden, and then, almost obscured by the haze, Q takes up the rear.

The ground is uneven, and with the varying width of the ledge, I have to work hard to fight my vertigo. I let my hand trail against the nearly black natural stone to my left. A pebble comes loose as I brush against it, bouncing on the ground by my feet before plummeting into the mist-filled depths. I hear it descending the cliff wall below us, each ricochet becoming fainter and fainter.

I never hear it hit the bottom.

When I look up, I see Cid's narrowed eyes. She's pissed at the noise I made, but she's going to have to live with it. I hear another pebble take a similar trek, disturbed by someone behind me. Maybe she and Q could do this quietly, but myself, Neb and Aiden just don't have those skills.

"How far up?" I ask so softly I'm half-mouthing the words to her.

"Miles," she answers, "and it will get much, much harder."

I take a couple steps and lean in, whispering into her ear. "Have you been here before?"

"No." I feel her warm breath on my cheek. "Not this exact place. But I've traveled this region before. If we're lucky, we won't have to climb much."

Considering the pebble I'd knocked loose just a moment ago, I do *not* think this wall is stable enough to climb.

"Cid!" My voice is a little too loud.

Neb's pretty close behind me now. We're holding everyone up.

Cid doesn't move yet, though. "This won't shake them, Cris. But it will slow them down. They probably don't have expert climbers with them."

Probably? Because Keith's guys are Cancer, one of them might have some infidel climbing training. Fucking Christ.

But that's not the worst part. "They'll be faster than us, Cid. They don't care if they die."

She nods. "Well, at least we all agree on something."

The ridge is a hellstone vein. That's how Cid knew it
would be here, and that's how she knew it would be
stable enough to walk on.

Infidels are so fucking brilliant sometimes.

The light has become dim in the thickening mists,
so unimaginably dim we can rarely see more than fifty
feet in front of us. Roots as giant as the ones we saw in
Dendra claw their way up through the earth, emerging
from the cliff wall in clumps. The roots often snake
around our ridge, occasionally breaking through the
hellstone vein we're on. In some places they make our
walk easier, giving us better footing. In others, they
make it much, much worse.

The roots themselves are slick both with condensation and with what seems like some kind of grey lichen. I step over one large gap, hoping against hope that the ledge is strong enough to hold me.

It is.

I see El Cid, a shadow in the fog, hopping over the next break. I can step across it, but Aiden won't be able to. Please, please, please, don't crumble.

I set my left hand against the cliff wall. I feel around until I find a jut that will serve as a handhold. There, that seems good. I test it twice, tugging hard to make sure it won't fall away. It seems okay. Then again, I might have just weakened it. I stretch one leg out, feeling the soreness in my hamstring. My foot finds purchase on the hellstone beyond. Then I finish the job, stepping across. Cid is waiting. I take a few cautious steps toward her.

Neb follows. Then he turns and holds up his arms.

Q picks up Aiden and hands him over to the necromancer.

El Cid touches my shoulder. "Come on."

In another hundred feet or so, the roots have torn away our ledge completely, and I can't see where it picks up again . . . if indeed it even does.

"Whisper what I say behind you," Cid tells me.

I turn as Neb catches up. "Whisper what I say behind you," I tell him.

He does so. I hear Aiden's tiny voice as he passes

the message on to Q.

Cid's warm breath is in my ear. "Put your hands where mine go. Put your feet where mine go too, if you can."

I turn and repeat the message.

When I look to Cid to get the next part, I see she's already got her back to me. Her tiny hands run across the wall.

If you can.

Because she's so small, I'll have difficulty copying her climb. I can certainly span her handholds, but if I try to mimic where she puts her legs, I'll get a little cramped.

Hell.

We're about to put Q's training to the test, but this situation is far from ideal. The wall is slick with the moisture of the air, and the cliff itself is made of hard-packed dark earth and loose stones ready to crumble away at any moment.

Cid begins.

I follow her as soon as I can, a hand here, and a hand there. I copy one of her footholds but have to improvise another. Aiden should have been behind her. Then Neb and I could have followed Q. That would have been wiser, all things considered.

My pack weighs heavily upon my shoulders. I feel some of my things shifting back there. God damn it.

I can't see where we're climbing to.

Cid stays just ahead of me, seemingly glued to the rock, careful, deliberate and calm. Maybe she's as scared as I am, but what does it matter? Infidels don't have to fucking act on their emotions.

And damn, you know what? I'm an infidel.

I don't have to be afraid. I can be calm.

The climbing becomes easy. It's like I'm locked in, hyper-focused. I have one thing to do. The fear melts off me. My breathing eases. The tiredness in my arms, it's an illusion created by the fear in my brain. I'm an infidel.

I hear Aiden's surprised grunt. A shower of pebbles rolls down the cliff behind me. I look back so fast I almost lose my grip. My heart is an insane thing, beating madly.

He's okay. He's got both his feet on what looks like a stable nook and he's feeling for a hold with his right hand along the dark grey wall.

Damn, damn, damn.

Whatever fucked up Zen I'd mustered a moment ago is gone. My hands shake as I try for the next hold. And the next, and the next.

El Cid makes a quick adjustment, moving from one set of holds to another in a single, quick motion. Fuck, I don't think I can do that. As I get there, though, I see I don't have to. My longer limbs let me take a smoother route. The wall is pretty much stone here. I realize the dirt we've been dealing with is just on top of the rock layer.

Then I hear something. It sounds like tiny clawing feet, reminding me of rats from the old world. El Cid's head jerks to one side, and she raises her left hand, motioning us to stop. I can't let go with my left hand to copy her, but the others aren't coming forward, so I can tell they got the message.

The clawing sounds are coming from below.

El Cid looks back, her mouth slightly open. She's scared. Cid is scared shitless.

Oh fucking God.

How many of the clawing things are there? What are they?

They're getting louder, which means they're getting closer. And we're trapped on this fucking rock face. Of all the luck.

El Cid's hand strays to the side of her pack, reaching into the pocket which I remembered her keeping infidel fire in.

The clawing continues, louder and louder. There could be a hundred of them, or a thousand, but there's definitely more than ten.

I peer down into the hazy depths. I see nothing. It feels like they're right there, right below us. Whatever they are, they'll be coming out of the mist. I can hear the trails of the dirt and stone they're displacing below us.

I secure a grip that will free my right hand, and then reach for my 9mm.

Balance first, then fire.

But if we start shooting, we'll draw the devils to us. In such an open area, there must be other groups within earshot.

Wait, are they getting farther away?

They are!

They fucking are! The scrapes of claws on rock and earth are getting softer.

And softer.

And softer.

And then all I can hear is the falling trails of dirt and stone.

El Cid begins moving again.

I remember the strange adjustment she made on the cliff face behind me. I'd been able to cross it, but would Aiden? He's shorter than Cid. Will he fall?

I have to keep up with her. I want to look back, but Cid's driving forward hard. She's found a root which runs up the side of the cliff.

She begins climbing it.

Not a bad idea.

I traverse the next few holds to make it to the root. It's only about a foot thick, and when I put my hands on it, I'm surprised by how slimy it is. How the hell is Cid climbing this thing?

At this point, the root has come free from the cliff, so I wrap my legs around it and shimmy. I quickly come to a point where it buries itself back into the wall.

I jam my hands into the dirt to get good traction. Then I continue.

I see a darker shadow in the mist. El Cid's heading toward it, so I think it must be a ledge.

It is! It's our ledge from earlier. But how had she known it would be here? Or did she just guess and luck out?

El Cid sends a shower of dirt down into the foggy abyss below as she crosses from the root to the ledge. See, Cid, you're not perfect.

But suddenly I wish she was.

The grade of the slope there is not too steep, which is probably why Cid chose that point to cross. Still, will the falling earth disturb the clawed devils we heard earlier? Will enough crumble away to make the root come loose and send us toppling down?

I cross to the ledge before my mind can imagine my fall.

It dawns on me how exhausted I am.

My arms are shaking, and I'm certainly out of breath. El Cid gives me a little room, so I use it to sit down.

When Neb comes I scoot over, not bothering to get to my feet. I do so again with Aiden's arrival, and then again with Q.

El Cid stands as we rest, one hand on her sidearm.

"How much farther?" I ask.

Cid shrugs. "Miles still. I've no way of knowing.

This vein should run us into a room I recognize. Then I can try to get us to Dendra. It's not taking us up as fast as I'd hoped, though, so it will be some time."

I think the mists have lessened a little. I can only see a hundred feet or so in either direction, but that's an improvement over fifty. Or I hope it is.

If we can see better, that means the devils can too. Will the clawed ones be able to spot us if they come that close again?

I hear something.

El Cid raises her hands.

It's another pebble, descending far, far below.

It's gone.

"The Carrion born have nearly caught up," Q says.

No.

He has to be wrong.

They can't have followed so far.

But Q isn't wrong about such things. And if they were going to get within earshot of us, it was going to be here. We might functionally be an hour ahead of them, but when our progress is so slow, an hour's travel might only be a quarter of a mile—or less.

I'm not so tired anymore.

I stand up. Aiden does too, and of course Q and El Cid are ready to go. Nebuchadnezzar, though, I don't think he's ready. He looks pale, like he's about to vomit.

"Neb," I tell him. "I questioned one of the Carrion born. He said Ryan had changed. Said he spent half his time as one person, and the other half as another."

His blue eyes focus on me. "What?"

"That's verification of a Revenant, Neb. It's what Cid said. Consistency and verification. Keith followed us onto Soulfall, and something came back with him in Ryan's body, but it wasn't Ryan."

Slowly, Nebuchadnezzar rises.

The mist may not actually be getting thinner, I realize. I can certainly see farther, but that might be because the world around me is getting brighter. The change is slight but noticeable. I remember, so long ago, looking down from Dendra into silvery mists. These must be those same mists, only we're much farther down.

We begin to see giant leaves in the haze overhead. Not the bright green broad leaves we saw in Dendra, but wrinkled, dark leaves that look almost like cooked spinach. They dangle from slick, grey branches which descend through the impenetrable grey sheets above.

"Here," Cid says, pointing to one such branch. "We begin."

I blink. "Begin?"

"Maybe we should stand and fight," I hear Neb suggest from behind us.

Poor Nazi. He's exhausted. He'd rather fight than climb if it means he'll get to sit down for a moment.

Cid ignores him. She takes us up one of those slippery grey branches. It's thin enough for me to wrap my legs around, so I shimmy up it. When we get to the main tree branches, climbing becomes even easier.

I hear Q's voice below me, a soft whisper of encouragement, as the Infidel Friend speaks to Neb. "This isn't the old world. There is a well of motivation within you, a store of adrenalin and sweat and blood which springs eternal. Your mind isn't built for that. It remembers how things were in the old world. It remembers when energy was finite. It remembers a place where infinite determination could not give you infinite motion."

I know these words.

He'd whispered similar ones in my ear once, when we were running from the City of Blood and Stone. I hope they work better for Neb than they did for me. The real problem is that they aren't quite true. There is no infinite will. On Earth, you could stay strong mentally even when your body quit. Hell doesn't really like that so much. It would rather pile your fatigue onto your will after it's worn out your muscles. That way it can break you completely in body and in spirit.

Cid takes us along one horizontal branch, and we're forced back into single file. I notice, for better or worse, that we end up in the same order.

The limb isn't quite as slippery as I'd feared. Maybe because the light is brighter, the lichen is having more difficulty growing. Who knows?

Our anemic branch is dipping now with our weight as we travel along it. I see other branches poking out toward us through the mist. After a moment, I realize those limbs are coming from another tree. Above us I can see the base of the second tree as it crawls downward out of the ceiling.

"Cid, why aren't we following the ledge?" I ask.

"Neb's too tired," she says. "And this path should help us stay ahead of the Carrion born. It's harder to track us in the trees."

"But what happens if we can't hop from tree to tree?"

She points down.

"Oh."

Our branch dips until it touches another limb from an upcoming tree.

"Hang on," Cid says. "Everyone lie down, hug the branch."

I follow her instructions, lowering myself to lay on my stomach while wrapping my arms and legs around the thick limb. I notice that the way I lay my head against the bark is the same way I'd lain my head against my opponents in wrestling training.

It's weird, the little things that stick with you.

Cid hops off the branch and it rises with a quick jerk. I can see why she had us lay down and hang on. The branch jumps again when I drop from it. Neb hands over Aiden, who I set down onto the new tree. Neb himself jumps shortly after, shaking our branch and slipping. Fortunately, with his arms wheeling, he regains his balance.

Q descends, landing lightly behind us, the branch barely swaying.

We'll never survive this. Not all of us, at least. Sooner or later, one of us is going to fuck up.

The canopy gets much thicker as we travel, and the leaves, though I'm not sure what light they have to sustain them, become full and broad like the ones we saw in Dendra. There are often multiple branches we can follow to get from tree to tree. That makes things much, much easier. As a bonus, these thicker limbs move less under our weight.

Cid's speed is increasing. She's gaining faith in our ability to follow her. She believes we're learning how to move through the trees. She may be right, but I know this is the time where I'm the most vulnerable. I'll start to relax, I'll think I know what I'm doing . . . and then I'll fall.

"The mist is thinning," I hear Neb warn from behind me.

Damn. He's right.

I can see pretty well now, perhaps a few hundred feet, although only the leaves closest to us are a vibrant green. Elsewhere, the haze saps away their colors until they look like soft, grey leaf-shaped cutouts. I turn, scanning the Hellscape around me. It's as if I'm in a bubble. The mists are moving, running quickly through the branches and around the tremendous gnarled tree trunks which descend from the ceiling. It gives me the impression that the tree we're on is sailing through the air. The canopy of these trees we travel upon form a sort of floor below us, the leaves rustling in the slight wind. Above us, the rock is tiered, broken up into roughly rectangular sections which rise higher and higher at a slight angle toward the edge of my vision. It is, in essence, an upside-down staircase for giants—and each step contains a small, downward-growing forest of over-sized trees.

Climbing that is going to be impossible. We'd have to scale a cliff, and then somehow climb along the ceiling like an ant, and then go up another cliff, and so on and so on.

Cid had better have a damn good plan for that.

I see tiny, flittering grey shadows with our increased visibility. They're birds, darting in and out of the branches. No danger there, I don't think.

Cid said we'd run into devils. If it's going to happen, it's probably going to happen here where the visibility is so much higher.

As we travel I see a tremendous spiderweb stretching across from one tree to another. It is perhaps two hundred yards at its widest point.

Its owner is home, standing near the center of the geometric web, its eight legs glinting in the dim light.

It's a silverleg spider. A giant silverleg spider. I didn't even know that could happen.

I'd met some of the tinier versions of this thing. Nasty buggers. Their legs are made of little needle-like metal blades. They have a spur in the bottom which will stick into your flesh. This one, though, is larger than an elephant, its legs the size of lances, its spurs the size of sickles.

Cid's pace increases ever so slightly.

I try to focus on the branch in front of me, but I keep checking on that silver bastard. It's moving now. Even from across the gulf that divides our trees, I can see it's not putting its pointed legs straight down into the web. Rather, it places the sides of its legs against its web, using the adhesive for traction.

Q is focused on the spider, so I force myself to pay more attention to where I'm putting my feet.

If it comes for us, Q will let us know.

I have no idea what the fuck we'll do about it, but Q will let us know.

Then I see another web, higher up and ahead.

Oh hell.

It's not long before I start getting a better feel for the chamber. The steps of the upside-down giant staircase form a caldera—or at least that's what I assume from the curve of the steps above. I still haven't seen the far wall.

"You sure Dendra is up there?" I whisper.

Cid nods. "Yes, in one of the chambers at the top."

There is a peculiar tree, a different breed than the rest perhaps, in the thirty or so to our right growing down from the tier we're on. The tree's leaves look the same, but the branches are heavy with some large kind of golden fruit.

Cid freezes.

Not fruit.

Those are imps, or as the infidels call them, pigmiditz—the things we'd faced when we'd rowed through Portsmouth. Thousands and thousands of them, weighing down the limbs.

"Two groups of the Order behind us, Cid," Q says. "They haven't spotted us yet, but it's not going to take them long."

I look back into the trees and mists. I can't see them. Maybe it's because I'm just a little too far forward and I have that extra bit of fog to look through—or maybe Q's just amazing like that.

Cid picks up the pace, and we're almost walking at a normal speed across the wide branches.

Our haste doesn't bother me when the limbs are ten

feet wide, but soon we step onto some which are only two or three, and it freaks me the fuck out. I see more webs, and more of the pigmiditz filled trees.

If we don't get through here soon, and the haze keeps clearing, things are going to blow up on us.

"I need another wrap," Neb says.

Cid shakes her head. "Give him one, Q, but Neb, don't take it yet."

Something's just gone more wrong. I can't tell from my senses, but I know Cid and I can feel her anxiety.

"The Carrion born have spotted us," Q says.

Cid changes our direction, cutting across some branches I hadn't expected her to take, bringing us around a fifty foot wide trunk. The steps in the ceiling get steeper ahead, and I can only see the tips of a few trees coming down from beyond our step's ledge. Past that, just a grey abyss. To our right, a giant silverleg spider crawls across its web. The next tree past that is one of those laden with pigmiditz.

Cid kneels by a knot in the trunk, and then peeks around it. "Some of the Carrion born got ahead of us."

How? How the fuck could they have done that?

"Let's take 'em out," Q says.

Cid drops back down, shaking her head.

I come up to the knot and look.

I don't see them at all. "Where?"

Sweat drips down from my eyebrow into my eye, the salt stinging me. I blink it away.

Cid's chest is rising and falling fast. "The tree ahead and to the left. They're in the lower branches."

I thought I'd looked there.

I look again.

Fuck. She's right. Of course she's right.

Keith's friends had to have known a shortcut because those fuckers are dug in.

Q's kneeling, his M-16 raised to his shoulder, looking back along the way we've come.

Now I see the groups Q said were behind us. They're perfectly dressed for the mist, their dark clothes allowing them to blend in. Damn, one of those groups is only three trees back.

"Pincer," Neb says.

"I can try and swing around," Q says. "Attack those ahead of us, clear our way while you guys hold off the others from behind."

There might be twenty in the group back there. This is not going to be good.

"I'll go," Aiden says.

Q absently rubs his bald head. "They're allied with the Order. They might have altered munitions."

"Do you have a choice?" My son's voice is calm.

Do we? Fuck yes we do.

"Infidel fire," I say.

Cid shakes her head. "That's going to be a hell of a throw, and I'm not sure if I can time it well enough to get them."

I think of the tree full of pigmiditz. "You don't really have to hit them, Cid."

Q whistles. "He's right, Cid. You just have to get that fire close. The pigs will launch themselves at our enemies. We can come around from there," he says, pointing to one tree, "to there," he points to another, "and then climb up. We have to be getting close to Dendra."

Cid bites her lip. "Hell."

Aiden's black eyes look toward the Carrion born.

"Not much time, Cid," I say.

Calmly, she removes a canister from the side of her pack. She steps away from the knot and moves to an open part of the branch. Her eyes close for a moment.

"Should Q throw it?" I ask.

She shakes her head. "You'll see. Stand clear."

That's going to be a hell of a throw. It might actually explode closer to our tree than theirs, which would *not* be helpful.

She squats a little, and holds her arms out wide. Her face is turned, looking back over her left shoulder. Her profile is striking. The ever so slight upturn of her nose, her angled jaw. The wisp of hair which falls down by her ear before curling around the base of her chin. Then she spins. It's like she's about to throw a discus. She takes a set of spiraling steps back toward the knot, all that momentum building up—then she releases and the canister sails into the air across the bottomless gulf between our trees. I hear just the faintest whine of the infidel fire as it flies through the abyss. She must have just barely unscrewed the cap.

We duck, not because we fear the blast, but so the pigmiditz don't see us.

The whine picks up volume and then, at its apex, goes quiet.

The explosion tears apart the silence. A ball of fire engulfs the lower branches of that far off tree. We hear a shriek as a Carrion born falls. Birds take flight, chirping fiercely, darting away.

For a moment, the silence returns. Then I hear the clicking sounds of thousands of pigmiditz. Their distant tree becomes a mass of molten gold as they come alive.

XXV

The first imp drops, headfirst from its bat-like perch, away from the stirring tree. It plummets downward, picking up speed before spreading its wings and leveling out. It glides now, crossing the divide, barely losing altitude. One of the Carrion born leaves the knot he's using as cover, raising his shotgun. I reach for my Old Lady, but Cid raises a hand to stop me.

She's right, no need to give up our position.

I look back to the imp tree.

Oh God.

I can't believe there are so many.

A steady stream of pigmiditz descends like the coming of a biblical plague. Some swoop to one side or the other before readjusting their flight toward the Carrion born's tree. The grey air is filled with the three foot golden beasts.

Fly, my pretties.

I hear the Carrion man's shotgun boom. The lone imp at the head of the rush seems unaffected for a second before tilting slightly downward. It tips farther and farther, until it's diving into the colorless abyss.

The Carrion born men are shouting to each other. They are climbing higher in the tree, trying to get over to a nearby set of branches. Two more shots ring out, but I know the oncoming wave must have more devils than the Carrion born have bullets.

"Those damn pigs are too low!" Neb whispers harshly.

And it looks like he's right, like they'll miss the Carrion born's tree altogether.

"Watch," Q says softly.

The imps pull up, their bat-like wings spread wide, their momentum carrying them upward. Then, just as they reach the point where their momentum stalls out altogether, they alight on the branches. The gunfire from the Carrion born grows more and more frantic. One branch cracks under the weight of a pigmiditz mass and breaks off, spinning down into the haze, shucking off the three foot golden devils as it falls.

I look behind us. The closest of the two Carrion groups coming up from the rear is only two trees back.

"Not much time!" I warn.

But Cid's hand stays up.

We're probably in range now. The Icanitzu armor will protect us, surely, but this is not a good place to be.

But maybe that's the point. If we can convince that group of Carrion born to fire at us, they'll become targets too. And they're just suicidal enough to do it.

I look back again to the imp tree.

Dear God, they're still coming.

The branches of the Carrion born's tree are now weighed down with the devils. One darkly dressed man, sword in hand, is courageously standing on a branch, slicing down the arriving imps.

A few of the golden devils have climbed above him. At first I think they'll get to spring their ambush, but his friends, though busy climbing to another tree, take the time to shoot the devils down.

The stream seems to be thinning out now, and the pack of pigmiditz is in a race, trying to catch up with the fleeing Carrion Born.

Good luck, little piggies.

El Cid's hand drops.

We move.

She takes us around the trunk so the Carrion born behind us very nearly have a clear shot. A few of them take it. A bullet slaps the trunk beside me, sending chunks of bark into the air.

El Cid, light on her feet, dances around to another

branch. I follow, a clumsy yet quick oaf, trying to keep pace with her. We get to the far side of the trunk. More bullets zip into the tree behind us. One of the giant leaves beside me is suddenly peppered with lead.

Hell.

Cid is eyeing a long branch.

She raises her hand.

Fuck.

There are shouts from the Carrion born tree ahead. The lone heroic swordsman still lags behind his friends. A pack of the imps had climbed the tree up to its roots and are now swooping down around him.

He misses a step, toppling into the mists.

More gunfire.

Another stream of pigmiditz has taken flight. Not toward us, toward the Carrion born group behind us, but a few of them are going to come damn close.

Cid draws her gladius. I feel behind my back for mine, finding the hilt. I draw it.

The golden devils soar by. One's beady little black eyes spot us, but he's a slave to his momentum, so onward he goes.

Cid breaks into a sprint.

Oh no fucking way can I go that fast.

I stand up and move after her. The branch wobbles under my feet. Bullets whiz through the air, though I'm not sure if any were actually aimed at me.

I cannot fall. I will not fall.

I just have to focus on the branch. I can't care about the rest of the battlefield. I just have to—I look up to Cid.

She's about to jump to the next tree.

God damn it.

She leaps and the limb shifts beneath me. I lose my footing and fall, nuts first, onto the branch, and catch on to the damn thing with my free hand.

Mother fucker.

I put my hand on the branch along with the fist which holds my gladius. I stand up as quickly as I can.

I think I'm okay.

An imp is heading right toward me. I go to slash it, but my abdomen thinks differently. I drop to my knees and vomit. The little devil shoots over my head. My bile coats the branch, parts of it dribbling down the side. I rise, but can't stand up all the way.

"Puke!" I warn with a strangled voice. "Don't step."

I cross over my own bile and try to catch up with Cid.

She's already on the next branch, heading to another tree.

I collapse at the trunk and vomit again. Q and Neb pull me to my feet.

We move again in single file as we leave the central branches. Cid is there, waiting for me at a tree whose limbs barely make it down to our level. She wraps her legs around one of the branches and climbs upward.

Fuck. I don't know if I can do this. I clutch a nearby limb and try to make my ascent.

Q helps Aiden up. Neb is swallowing his wrap—that's his second.

My body tries to vomit again, but there's nothing left.

I climb as I dry heave.

Cid has stopped at a main branch near the bottom of the tree. She's looking upward along the trunk, eyes wide.

The flat ceiling above us gives way to a cliff which soars almost straight up. Trees hang like upside down bonsai, forming nice little organic ladders we can use. The effect is awe inspiring. The space above us is like a mile-wide chimney. So many of those trees have clusters of pigmiditz—and worse.

A giant silverleg spider climbs across the tree's trunk above us, its spurs ripping out tiny pieces of bark as it moves.

It stops, then spins, its myriad legs pumping, their points raining chunks of wood down upon our shoulders.

Its twin conglomerations of reflective black eyes stare directly at us.

"Torch!" Cid yells.

"Don't have one!" Q shouts back.

"Damn it," Cid curses, reaching into her pouch. "Cover!"

But there is nowhere to take cover.

She tosses the canister up and I hear the high whistle. Cid drops and shields her head with her arms.

Right, the infidel armor.

I do the same, but Aiden doesn't. He stares toward his fate.

The explosion goes off. A piece of shrapnel has lodged itself into Aiden's cheek, and black blood is pouring from it. He seems unaffected, but how had the metal cut him? He's supposed to be immune.

Shit, the infidel fire canisters must be made from hell stuff. The shrapnel can hurt him. It can pierce my armor.

The silverleg spider is running away, but if it's injured, I can't tell.

"They fear fire!" Cid shouts.

She takes us up the tree through the explosion's smoke, finding handholds in the bark, and on occasion, in the indentions left by the legs of the spider.

But the spider is too fucking stupid. As we climb higher, it comes around from the other side of the tree. It just ran all the way around. The spider stops again, just a bit below us, when it comes back to where the blast occurred. It backs away from the fire-scarred trunk, but appears not to see us. Neb, who's at the rear, is only ten feet above it. He freezes.

So do I.

Then the silverleg charges downward, away from us.

I see some Carrion men emerging from the canopy below.

Unlucky fuckers.

We continue. The sounds of gunfire and screams come up from the abyss.

We come to where our tree's root system spreads out into one of the tiered ceilings. Cid starts climbing along a root that will take her horizontally across the stone roof to the edge. She does so, upside down, similar to how I had shimmied up the branch earlier, her hands and legs somehow finding purchase in the contours of the wood and earth. I look to where she's headed and see more branches dangling down from beyond the upward step, their leaves longer than a man is tall.

I sure as hell don't want to follow her.

A flicker of light in my peripheral vision catches my attention.

I look back through the thinning mist.

About a quarter of the way around the next tree, metallic legs flashing in the light, come perhaps fifty or so giant spiders.

Oh fucking Jesus Christ.

Beyond them I see the streams of imps coming toward us, not from just one tree, but from four or five—of course, they saw our explosion. With any luck they're headed toward the Carrion born further down our trunk.

"Cid!" I yell, pointing to the masses.

"Move!" she shouts back, not even looking.

My pack shifts as I grab onto the root above me. I feel its weight tugging me down. I jam my hands into the dirt on either side. In certain places, the root comes out of the ceiling, making it easier to grip.

Nothing in Q's climbing training was anything like this. I raise my legs and put one foot against the oversized trunk. I bend my other leg, trying to hook it around the underside of the root.

I hear more gunfire below.

My foot slips and my legs fall, wheeling in the open air below me.

My hands are nearly ripped from the root.

I'm screaming.

I think I sprained my wrist. Fuck.

This is not good.

You have to work, wrist. I will not fall.

Fuck my legs. Let them hang.

The world swims before me. The imps flow in below us, a steady stream, some of them falling out of the air to the gunfire of the Carrion born. A couple of enemy explosions go off, sending hordes of imps careening out of the sky.

The blasts force their silverleg spider back up at us.

There's no time for me to be careful. If I fall, I fucking fall.

I twist with a quick motion, and then, like an insane man on monkey bars, I reach out one arm and swing toward Cid. My own momentum pushes me up a little, and I jam my wounded wrist into the earth by the root. Without stopping to worry about the shockwaves of agony streaming into my brain, I let go with my good hand and swing again. And I grab and swing again, and again. It gets easier toward the edge as the thickness of the root decreases.

"Grab my leg!" Cid yells.

I do, and somehow she's strong enough to lift us both onto the branches. I let go of her and cling to one of the limbs.

Like a monkey, Cid shoots up into the next tree. I see where she had posted her other foot in the cliff in order to lift me.

"Grab my leg!" I shout down behind me, finding a handhold at the beginning of a leaf's stem and bracing myself on the cliff wall.

Ever so slightly, the branch sways. Jesus.

Aiden grabs my leg. How the hell did he get in front of Neb?

I lift him easily. Neb must be next. But then, how will he get up? Aiden won't be able to help him.

"Go!" I shout to Aiden.

My boy follows Cid.

I lower myself back down. "Grab my leg!"

Two of Neb's arms wrap around my leg. It's harder to lift him, but I manage. I follow after my son, no longer worried much about falling.

"Grab my leg!" I hear the necromancer's voice calling out from below.

He must be shouting to Q. Did we all make it? Holy shit!

Can we do that again? How many more times will we have to?

There is a pause in the gunfire from the Carrion

born in the tree we just left, and I have no idea if that's a good thing or not.

God damn.

The climbing gets harder as we near the top of this new tree. My wrist seems better. I look and see it's swollen, though. Shit. I guess I just can't feel it. At least my grip is still strong. That's something.

This tree's base is right at the edge of one of the stepped ceilings, and the branches of the next tree intermingle with its roots—which makes for an easy climb.

Thank God for that.

I pass Aiden by, going quickly up one of those root-entangled branches. Maybe I can catch up to Cid.

The next trunk above us is over three hundred feet tall. This, though, is going to be a hell of a climb.

As I come up through the lower canopy, I realize the roots above are going to be too thick for the climbing method we'd used before. Cid's at those roots now, tying something off with string.

"Cris!" Neb shouts.

I look down to him. He's pointing toward the far wall, so I turn to take in the wide chamber.

Shit, a pigmiditz stream is heading right toward us.

I climb faster. There's just nothing else I can do. The bark handholds allow for good speed, but I have no idea if it will be enough.

"Cid, we're fucked!" I scream.

"Keep going!" she yells back.

The string she's tying up is far too thin to hold my weight, and the roots are too thick for me to wrap my arms around.

"Go!" she shrieks, manically working at something she's burying into the roots.

Fuck, that's infidel fire.

I shove both my hands into the earth on one side of the root since I cannot reach both sides at once. My grip holds my weight as my feet dangle. Below me, I see waves of the pigmiditz we'd left behind crawling from our previous ledge into the lower canopy of our current tree. With a strength I'm not sure will be sufficient, I reach out with my right hand and jam it in farther over. Then I catch up with my left. My feet wheel beneath me, and my grip slips an inch. Maybe if I keep moving, I won't fall.

Right hand, swing and pull, left hand.

Right hand, swing and pull, left hand.

Right hand, swing and pull, left hand.

"Hang onto me!" Q is shouting to Aiden.

Q's long arms let him go much faster than me. He, and Aiden, who clings around his waist, pass by me on another root.

Neb is following on mine, slower than even myself.

Cid is still fiddling with the infidel fire on the far side of the tree.

Right hand, swing and pull, left hand.

The glints of silver are on the edges of my vision again, but this time from below. Even if we make it to the next tree, it won't matter. The imps can climb the ceilings and catch up. Hell, the silverlegs can too. The issue here is that all of our enemies are faster than us.

But there's nothing I can do.

I probably shouldn't look down.

Right hand, swing and pull, left hand.

I look.

The silverleg spiders are pouring up onto the cliff below us. Golden-skinned imps are landing in our tree, joining the climbing hordes of their brethren giving chase from below. One of the highest tries to swoop up into me directly. He hits the ceiling to my right and falls back down, followed by clods of dirt. Holy hell.

Here's to hoping they're not smart enough to fly in above us and cut us off.

I come to the edge, but the branch is too far away for me to reach. There's no way forward. I stop, forcing Neb to halt as well.

"I'm slipping!" he shouts. "Move!"

But there's nowhere to go. Another imp swoops up at me, just coming short of my boot before gliding away into the hellacious chamber.

"Go back!" I shout to Neb.

"What?"

Fuck. Cid's coming along our root, now, too.

I need to move. Never mind if I die later, at least let

there be a later. I may not be able to reach the branch, but the root curls up the cliff at the edge of the step. I pull myself up, trying to climb onto the next cliff. I can't, my arms are shaking, and I can't.

Desperately, I swing my legs up, trying to jam them into the root on the vertical face. No good. My feet aren't finding anything to catch.

"I'm slipping!" Neb's voice is frantic.

Fuck.

I hear rustling above. It's Q. He's in a branch swinging toward me.

I get my feet to stop wheeling and prepare to reach out, but the branch has swung away. My fingers start slipping. Suddenly I feel Neb's arms around me.

His weight adds to mine.

"No, Neb!" I yell. "No!"

My hands are almost loose, but Q's branch is there. I grab onto it, getting one arm around it and another arm around the base of one of the human-sized leaves.

I hear the branch crack under the weight of the three of us as we swing.

Q leaps off, catching onto another limb. Neb and I climb. I see where our branch is tearing slowly away from the main trunk. Fresh sap spills out from the broken portion of the limb. The wood is nearly white under the dark grey bark, and I realize it's too green to break cleanly. Our branch is going to rip down along the trunk before snapping off.

Frantically I fight my way around and through the giant leaves. I come to the break and grab onto the bark of the main trunk. Neb is right behind me. Cid comes around, ignoring the branches altogether, free climbing the cliff. Clods of dirt and stone fly away from her lightning fast holds and releases.

She leaps from the cliff to a horizontal branch, landing on her feet. Even as she does so, she releases a stone from her belt. It drops, and I see white lines of string falling with it.

"Up!" Her voice is desperate. "No time!"

Above us, up the narrowing chimney which seems to rise forever, I see circling swarms of imps.

They're coming.

"Higher!" Cid shouts.

I'm climbing as fast as I can.

"Timber!" Cid is yelling. "It's fucking going down."

Somehow, I find a bit more speed.

Oh shit, why do I hear whistling? Not just whistling, a chorus of high, angelic tones. The sound of a whole set of infidel fire screaming out at a siren's pitch in a single, simultaneous call.

A silverleg spider crests the cliff below, heading our way.

The tree shakes and the explosions thunder as fire balloons out, curling up the side of the cliff. Loose rock and clumps of root shoot out into the haze, tearing the fabric of the fog and swirling it about into tiny whirlpools. A wall of dust, dirt and stones, shaken free from the wall beside me, descends in a mass slowly into the abyss below — taking that spider with it.

I hear a horrible cracking. It's the wood, and then comes a sound of rustling so loud it seems like an entire forest is falling.

Imps fill the air below the cliff ledge, fleeing from the falling tree. Then I see the tree itself, covered in masses of golden pigmiditz, Carrion born, and silverleg spiders, descending down into the grey abyss.

Cid has saved us again.

Now all we have to do is get through the thousands of circling imps above us.

"What are we going to do about the pigmiditz?" Q shouts.

I look up to the next stepped ceiling. There they are, climbing upside down along the roof.

Cid draws a pistol and starts shooting them down.

Damn.

That can't be a winning strategy.

"This way!" Cid shouts.

My arms aren't up for this. "I need a wrap!"

Q has paused on the wall, bracing himself with his feet. He's drawn his pistol and is firing with his left hand while his right dips into his pack. He drops the wrap.

I catch it and swallow it.

It's as bitter as I remember. More bitter than coffee grounds. More bitter than a fistful of pennies. More bitter than Myla's vile heart.

I feel my blood pumping immediately.

Cid has a plan. She has to have a plan.

She always has a plan.

The imps keep coming, and one's heading straight for me.

Jesus.

I draw my 9mm and start firing. The slight kick of the gun feels odd in my swollen wrist. The imp drops out of the sky.

My wrist has gotten worse, certainly, but I still can't feel any pain.

Please keep working.

The next step in the ceiling has enough flora on it to make it an easy climb, if it weren't for the imps.

Q takes out a canister of infidel fire and twists it. I hear the whistle, but he hasn't let it go yet.

Then he tosses it upward around the inverted ledge.

It explodes just past the edge of the cliff above us. I can't see any of the imps up there through the ceiling, but I see their dead comrades' bodies dropping.

"Now!" Cid yells.

Gun still in hand, she climbs along the horizontal root. She starts firing as she comes to the ledge. She puts one leg up, wrapping it around a branch from the next step. Her empty clip drops away as she reloads. She continues firing as she swings up, disappearing behind the edge.

The imps keep falling as I approach, and I hear her pistol's reports suddenly replaced by an M-16. I crest the edge using a tree branch and climb up next to Cid.

She's found a hellstone ledge along this cliff, similar to the one we'd traveled before.

"Hold them off!" she shouts, jumping to the ledge. "Then follow me!"

I draw the Old Lady and fill the air around me with bursts of buckshot as Aiden crests the edge.

"Move!" I say as I fire the last shell.

I toss out one of my own canisters of infidel fire at the oncoming imps, and instantly regret my decision. The shock isn't going to make climbing any easier.

The whistle is its own warning, though.

I grab Neb as it explodes, the blast going off a little lower than I meant it to, but the fire and smoke is enough to slow the devils.

Q comes up.

Cid's running along the ledge, but fuck, she's not going up. She's going right toward a tree full of spider webs. We follow.

A silver leg spider is charging at Cid.

She reaches into her pouch but comes up empty. "I'm out!"

She moves back, and I ready my second canister.

Three of the thing's legs are walking along the ledge, but the others are digging into the wall beside it.

She runs into Aiden and only her preternatural grace keeps her from falling. She slips around him, recovering her balance.

Aiden stands still, looking at the oncoming spider.

I draw my M-16.

The silverleg spider comes to a sudden halt, freezing before my son.

Aiden takes a step toward it, his arm raised.

He's fearless . . . and he should be. The spider and he have more in common than he and I.

One of the thing's silver legs rises, as if trying to keep Aiden at bay.

I start firing. So does Q.

It flees up the side of the cliff.

My shots stray high, and some of my bullets hit the wall rather than the spider.

This is far more effective than I thought.

In an unlucky rockslide, the spider tumbles, bouncing off a branch and disappearing into the canopy below.

Q is still shooting, aiming out into the chamber.

I look back to see a fresh wave of pigmiditz coming at us.

The ledge isn't really wide enough to run, but we do our best.

Cid's rummaging through her pack as she moves, pulling out a blanket.

The tree we're heading to, hell, that entire section of the wall, is covered in webs and giant silverlegs.

She's got her blanket on fire somehow.

Ten or so silverlegs are coming out to meet us, but they stop when confronted with her flaming blanket, now wrapped around her gladius. She waves them back as we enter under the strands of the web, but I notice she's careful not to get her improvised torch too near the spider silk

The imps are soaring in, but as we get deeper into the maze of webs, they start getting caught in the filaments.

I knew it. I knew Cid had a plan.

The silverlegs draw away from Cid's fire at first, but after a while, they ignore us altogether in favor of the masses of pigmiditz caught amidst the three foot thick silken strands.

"Don't touch the web," Cid says. "When the web shakes, the spiders are attracted to that point. This way."

Cid's fire is almost out as we come to another web-covered tree. We climb it. She said not to touch the spiderwebs, but they're impossible to avoid entirely. Even when we don't, the branches attached to the web are shaking it.

The effect isn't good, we've recaptured the attention of some of the spiders.

Cid ushers us past her.

We are just above most of the webs. I look back to see Neb, Q and Aiden climbing. Cid lowers her dying torch, touching it against a strand.

"Hold your breath!" she's shouting.

The conflagration is amazing.

I close my eyes as the world around me turns to smoke. I feel a hand against my shoulder. I'm being tugged onward.

My heart pounds, but I don't dare open my mouth for air.

I try opening my eyes, but the smoke is too much. I can't see shit, and the heat alone is enough to blind me. I must be on fire.

The tug is more insistent.

I can't fucking climb blind.

But I try.

I feel desperately along the contours of the branch, finding handholds. Up I go. Slowly, but up I go.

My heart is beating way too fast. My lungs contract, and I hear my own chest's attempt at a gasp. I have to breathe. My hands are shaky.

I inhale.

Now I'm coughing. My head spins. I keep going.

"Breathe, Cris!" A shout comes.

But I can't. I try but I can't.

Everything is hazy.

Am I holding onto the branch? Am I not?

I cough and cough.

Q's got me. His arm is around me. Neb is lying on a ledge above.

I cough more.

It doesn't feel like I'm breathing. Each time I try to get more air, my lungs reject it. Even so, I'm starting to see more clearly—except for the stars in my vision.

The mist has been replaced by the smoke.

Fuck it. I can climb.

I move toward Neb.

Aiden is beside him, seemingly unfazed.

"Keep near the smoke," Cid's voice is hoarse. "It's cover."

Gunfire and explosions start again below us. There must be some Carrion born left back there, fighting for their lives. They'd probably be dead already if we weren't causing so much destruction up here.

We climb along with the smoke, hoping against hope that it gives us some cover. Even as it swirls upward, the imps spiral downward, heading to either the firefight with the Carrion born or to the fires Cid had caused in the trees below. I look up, and no longer see any of the stepped tiers. It's just one giant chute now, with scattered trees bravely growing from juts in the wall.

Sounds echo oddly as we ascend through this giant chimney. In some places, it's as if the firefight is right by us, but in other places, it seems like it's more distant.

The mist increases in thickness, taking the place of the dwindling smoke, and I begin to feel safe again. We start crawling on veins of bright skystone and light rock. At times they cast our shadows deep into the mists. That can't be good, but the devils don't seem to see us.

Then Cid stops everyone. "I'll be back with rope."

With rope?

Where's she going to get that?

I look to Q.

He grins. "I think she's right. I think we're below Dendra."

A rope falls nearby me.

"Cid!" I shout.

It's Amirani who comes down it, though.

"Come on!" the infidel says. "Move quickly. We've got to rush your son through the city."

"Should we climb around Dendra?" I ask.

He shakes his head. "Dendra's at a choke point, remember?"

That's right, it takes two days to get around. Amirani climbs up out of my vision. I follow.

My right hand's grip isn't strong enough to hold my weight.

Fuck.

Well I'm glad it lasted this long.

I run the rope through my crotch, cross my legs, and get Jessica's shoes on either side of it. Then I push up with my legs. Left hand, push. Left hand, push.

Below me, Neb, Aiden and Q climb onto the rope.

I can barely see through the silvery mists as we ascend. The rope is flush with the wall, allowing everyone to propel themselves upward with their feet. Everyone but me. Since my hands can't alternate as my feet work, the wall does me no good.

"Sorry," I say about my slow pace.

"Don't worry," Amirani says. "Most of the creatures won't be able to get up here. You should be safe. I've seen some of the Order pass through the city, though, so you'll probably have a fight waiting for you when you leave."

If we even get to leave. Dendra's going to be pissed we climbed up here with weapons—not to mention the fact that we're toting a wight.

The mists thicken enough to blind me altogether.

"Switch ropes!" Amirani calls.

It's a good warning. I would have been shocked when I come to where our rope ends. I find a second rope there, fastened to the cliff, and I start up it.

"How much farther?" Neb asks from below.

"Almost there," Amirani responds.

Then I see it, a horizontal branch cutting through the mists.

"No one lives in this tree," Amirani says. "Too many casualties because of the low visibility. There's only soldiers. Just follow me. Act like you know what you're doing and like you belong here. They're on alert because of the explosions, so they won't pay much attention to you unless you make them."

I climb upon the branch. It's only two feet wide, and it bows a little under my weight, but I lay down on it. I feel it dip as our friends join.

Cid is there, above me, smiling. "Get up, lover. We're not out of the woods yet."

I hope to God that pun was accidental. I rise, like an infidel rises, posting my one good hand and swinging one leg under me.

We walk toward the tree that grew the branch we stand on. When it's wide enough, Amirani passes by me.

He leads us up a set of bridges which circle around the trunk like a spiral staircase.

"Amirani and team," he calls up to the next tree. "Don't shoot."

"Understood," a man answers.

I follow Amirani and Cid, head bowed, as we pass up through the vine and branch bridges. There are soldiers in the lighter mist, kneeling, rifles and bows at the ready. They're looking at us. Beyond them the haze clears and I can see all of Dendra.

The upside-down trees cling to this, the ultimate

ceiling of the chamber we fought our way through, forming a small grove. Wooden walkways and wicker bridges line the limbs, sometimes spanning from tree to tree. Huts made of interwoven foliage nestle themselves into the nooks and crannies created wherever gnarled branches meet the irregular uber-oak trunks. Before I remember there being birds flying about, but not now. Smoke from the fires we'd set below dirties the last wisps of the remaining fog, the mixture blending together like smog over an old world city.

One of the wicker-helmed guards turns to Amirani. "Infidels?"

Amirani nods. "We don't have much time with the mists letting up. There are enemies below."

The treeman nods. "They can't have weapons in here, Amirani, you know that."

"Of course," he answers. "I need four of your men to carry their guns."

"Quickly," Amirani says to us. "Give up your weapons to these men. The faster you get through Dendra the better."

I touch Aiden's shoulder. "Keep your eyes down, son."

The man who comes up to me is distracted. His wicker helmet is askew, cocked to the right. His eyes look behind me, down to the mists. I don't think they're going to have time to search us. I pass him my pack, the Old Lady holstered in it, my M-16, and my gun belt.

However, I leave my .22 hidden in the small of my back.

I see the others have given their weapons up as well.

"Follow me," Amirani barks.

He's right to be nervous. Aiden is pretty clearly undead, and I remember the punishment for letting a wight into the city was death.

There is another explosion from below. Damn, some of those Carrion born are still alive, it seems.

I feel much more comfortable with my piece behind me. I almost reach out to touch it for assurance, but I stop myself. No point in calling attention to it.

I look out over the bridges and landings we'll cross to get to Dendra's exit.

The guards fall behind us as we push quickly by their perimeter and into Dendra proper. They don't seem worried, which is good. I keep my hand on Aiden's shoulder and guide him forward. I figure I'm as good an obstacle as any to block the guards' vision.

"Is it just the Order chasing you?" Amirani asks.

Cid casts a worried look below. "No, they're allied with some Carrion born. Igraine's people, specifically."

"Understood. Like I said, some have come through here. If you're right, Cid, and it's anything like an infused, it's going to follow you like a hound, but we'll try and hold his guys up here. You plan to take the Lethe to ditch him?"

Cid steps carefully off the knots which hold two

branches together, her hand firm on the railing. "No. The Kingsriver. We'll boat south. Maybe a long ways. As far as Macon's Bend if we have to."

Aiden's caution is lacking as he travels over the branches, but considering the circumstances, a death wish is the least of his worries.

"And if he stays on your tail?" Amirani asks.

She hops up a set of stairs carved into the trunk. "Then we'll head east, meet up with some infidels. Make a stand."

"I'm coming with you," Amirani says.

"Now's not the safest time to join us," I say.

He chuckles.

It's definitely not safe to travel this fast over the trees, but compared to that wicked climb earlier, this seems like an old world stroll.

We come to a wide landing. Our group moves past a few wicker-helmed soldiers. Despite our rush, they don't pay us any attention.

"They're reinforcements," Amirani explains after we pass them. "If fighting occurs at any point in our perimeter, they'll be called to bolster the defenses there."

We pass a woman carrying a sack full of sinfruit. Aiden bumps into her, and for a second, he looks up. She gasps.

I glance back at the soldiers.

No reaction yet.

"He's got his mother's eyes," I tell the woman.

She scurries by.

The soldiers watch her go, but appear oblivious. For her part, the woman must have figured they knew what was going on. We look mighty official with Amirani in the lead and our soldiers-cum-pack-mules in the back.

My heart pounds as we near the exit. I wish we didn't have to leave. I could use a good ten-hour nap right about now.

I call up to Cid. "How much more running will we have to do?"

She mounts the bridge which leads to Dendra's exit. "We have to make it back to Jessica, Jenner, Eagan and Mason. It won't be as long this time since we won't have to drop by the Pole. We can get a couple hours of sleep while they make the canoes . . . if they're still around after all this time."

If.

"Why is this thing following us?" I ask. "Why does it care?"

She shrugs.

Whatever its reasons had been, I'm guessing that now it has to be Aiden. I remember Callodax's strange gaze at my son through the crystal wall. My swollen hand aches as it forms a fist.

We're going to go out the same way we came in so long ago. I see a trio of psychopomp sparrows take flight and soar out across the unreal chamber, flitting between the unearthly branches.

I don't know if I can make this next run without another wrap—but I've had two already.

Wicker-helmed soldiers pour out of the entrance, bows raised, nocked and pointed toward us.

Amirani and Cid freeze.

"My god," Cid says. "It's him."

Keith walks out of the exit, his superman-esque hair marked still by that grey streak. Harris is at his right side.

"Unfortunate," Amirani says.

"You can't get away from me, Godslayer," Keith says, pausing to flash us a white-toothed smile. "These arrows have hellstone tips. They're made to fell Icanitzu and I have a feeling they'll cut through your boy."

Well *he* knows my son is a wight. My hand drops to my waist. If I'm fast enough, I can kill this fucker.

Cid raises her hands.

"The Tree Lord wants to see you, Amirani," Keith says, his grin spreading across his face, his eyes wild.

Something is wrong with Keith. He seemed so much more in control before, even after Soulfall. Callodax must have fucked with his mind, too.

How did he get ahead of us?

"Check the boy's eyes," Keith's voice cracks as he gives the order.

Aiden steps forward, unbidden, and looks at the

soldiers. I hear the creaking of their bows as a few draw their arrows back harder.

My hand clutches the handle of my gun.

"Take them to the Wicker Tree," Keith orders. "Except the boy, he stays with me."

I cock back the hammer.

The soldiers move forward, but Amirani raises his hand. "Belay that. The boy goes to the Wicker Tree with the rest."

Keith smirks. "The laws are quite clear, my Lord."

I pull out my pistol and point it at Keith. His smile intensifies, and he almost seems relieved. My God, he wants me to kill him.

"Hold," Amirani's voice booms. "These men and the wight go to trial. Those are Dendra's laws. There's no law saying that you should give up a wight to the Order."

The soldier's bows are trained on me. Keith's chest rises and falls.

Aiden stands like a marble statue, arms wide, fearless.

I feel Cid's hand on my shoulder. "If we fight, we all die. At best, you'll kill Keith. It's not worth it."

"They'll yield," I whisper.

She shakes her head.

"This isn't the kind of thing you can be logical about!" I shout.

"Do you love me?" she asks.

My jaw slackens.

"Trust me." Her green eyes seem very sad. "We have a chance with a trial. None if we fight." She turns to Amirani. "We surrender and throw ourselves upon your justice."

I offer up my pistol, handle first. I'm so tired.

So fucking tired.

Wicker-helmed men come over, tentatively, step by step. I realize I'm holding the weapon in the infidel grip which will allow me to fire it should I need to. I look at Cid. One man takes away my gun. Others begin patting us down, their rough hands slapping against me. Keith laughs and laughs and laughs.

His laughter becomes higher and higher pitched, and it's hard now to tell if Keith is laughing or crying — if he's triumphant or insane.

What's happened to him?

"What the fuck have you done, Keith?" Cid asks him. "What did you bring back? How could you be so fucking careless?"

The guards grab us and start pulling us away.

I can see the sorrow in Keith's eyes, the hatred, the desperation. He opens his mouth as if he's about to speak, but nothing comes out. Poor bastard is as fucked as we are.

"Help us," I shout, resisting my guard's pull. "Help us, Keith, we can protect you from it!"

Keith lowers his eyes and says nothing, reminding

me of how insane Fin had been while we'd held him in the complex.

I shake myself free. "Help us! You know he'll kill you. He'll do worse than kill you. It's your fault, Keith. That shit is on you! Do you know where he's from?"

The guards stop, staring at him.

Keith's shaking, his eyes glistening as if he's holding back tears.

Then he looks at me, this man, my mortal enemy, seeming for all the world like a lost child. "I'm sorry, Godslayer," he says. "I'm so sorry."

Want to be notified when sequels are released? Register as a Citizen at hellsongseries.com

Need to look up a term?
Check out the Gehennic Encyclopedia as a free download on Kindle or view at our website: hellsongseries.com/encyclopedia

Sisyphean
Publishing

Hellsong Series

What is it like to be damned?

Arturus knows.

Born in Hell, Arturus has never had the chance to meet his creator or seek redemption; but that doesn't mean he has no destiny. He lives near the village of Harpsborough, whose people have torn a moment of peace from the unwilling claws of damnation—and damnation wants it back.

Future omens are poor. Infidels roam the wilds, devils are amassing, and the very stones of Hell themselves have begun to break apart. But even while they fight damnation, Arturus and the hunters of Harpsborough find themselves facing off against traitors from amongst their own ranks and a people they thought they'd left far behind.

Look for *Even Hell Has Knights* and continue exploring the Hellsong Universe!

Hellsong Series

Like a character? Want to follow them through the Hellsong universe?

Cris returns in *Execution*.

Cris appears in *Even Hell Has Knights* and *March till Death*.

El Cid, Q and Aiden appear in *Knight of Gehenna* and *March till Death*

A Note from Sipub

Did you enjoy this book? If you did, please keep in mind that we are a small press. Sisyphean Publishing does not have the marketing dollars to match a "big five" or mainstream publisher. We rely on you, our reader, to spread the word about our amazing tales.

So if you would, take a moment to leave a review at your relevant point of sale, share your thoughts about this novel with a friend, and/or make the appropriate sacrifice/propitiation/prayer to your deity of choice (except for *Kurtulmak*, that would just be awkward) on our behalf!

Sincerely,

Michael Cannon
Director of Distribution
Sisyphean Publishing

Shaun McCoy lives in South Carolina. He is an accomplished Pianist, Cage Fighter, Chess Player and Writer. You can check out his fan page at www.facebook.com/shaunomccoy